MW00744267

.

Barcelona Tales

Aliette de Bodard   Alberto M. Caliani

Claude Lalumière   Virginia Pérez
de La Puente

Sofia Rhei   Sarah Singleton

Lisa Tuttle   Ian Watson

Ian Whates   Marian Womak

One of a Special Signed Hardback Edition
Limited to just 50 numbered copies
This is number:

37

Barcelona Tales
Edited by Ian Whates

NEWCON
PRESS

NewCon Press
England

First edition, published in the UK November 2016
by NewCon Press

NCP 107 (hardback)
NCP 108 (softback)

10 9 8 7 6 5 4 3 2 1

Compilation copyright © 2016 by Ian Whates
Introduction copyright © 2016 by Ian Whates

"The Translator" copyright © 2016 by Lisa Tuttle
"Secret Stories of Doors" copyright © 2016 by Sofia Rhei
"Catacomb Saints" copyright © 2016 by Dave Hutchinson
"A Tale of No City" copyright © 2016 by Rodolfo Martínez
"The Ravisher, The Thief" copyright © 2016 by Marian Womack
"Himmler in the Barcelona Hallucination Cell" copyright © 2016 by Ian Watson
"Dark Pages" copyright © 2016 by Ian Whates
"Children of the Black Lady" copyright © 2016 by Virginia Pérez de La Puente
"Equi Maledicti" copyright © 2016 by Sarah Singleton
"The Dance of the Hippacotara" originally appeared at *Lost Myths*, 20 April 2010,
copyright © 2010 by Claude Lalumière
"There Will Be Demons" copyright © 2016 by Alberto M. Caliani
"What Hungers in the Dark" copyright © 2016 by Aliette de Bodard
"Barcelona/My Love" copyright © 2016 by Elia Barceló

All rights reserved, including the right to produce this book, or portions
thereof, in any form.

ISBN: 978-1-910935-27-9 (hardback)
978-1-910935-28-6 (softback)

Cover design copyright © 2016 by Ian Whates
Based on a photograph by Manuel Franco Arrabal
Text layout by Storm Constantine

Contents

Barcelona Tales:
An Introduction

Ian Whates

Native English speakers are notoriously lazy. Much of the world speaks English, so why bother learning another language? I'm as guilty as most: a smattering of French and German, enough Spanish to order a coffee, and that's about it... Which is a shame, because there's a wealth of literature, of stories and wonderment, which never gets translated into my native tongue and, as a result, many of us are oblivious to.

Spain has a thriving genre community, with writers producing first rate SF and fantasy, but how many people in the UK or the USA have ever heard of the authors involved, let alone read them?

2016 sees Barcelona stage the annual European Science Fiction Convention Eurocon, and that seemed a perfect opportunity to showcase some of Spain's finest genre authors in a way that might introduce them to a new readership. I must emphasise that this is not a crusade; I have no intention of forcing anything on anyone or demanding attention from any quarter; it's simply a means to facilitate a process that has been going on for centuries: new readers discovering new authors.

Barcelona Tales features a collection of stories set in or inspired by Catalonia's jewel of a city, written by authors from several countries: Spain, Britain, France, and Canada. I am humbled by the knowledge that many of the Spanish contributors have written their stories in English rather than having them translated, and must give a special mention to

Aliette de Bodard, who delivered her tale as promised despite having recently become a mother for the second time, with all the time pressures that involves. I am delighted by the quality and variety of the stories that have resulted. Barcelona as she has never been portrayed before. The book is here to be enjoyed. I can only hope you do so.

Ian Whates
Cambridgeshire
September 2016

The Translator

Lisa Tuttle

Sallie (Louise) Crowl *(b. 1961, Cleveland, Ohio) American novelist. Early works (as by S.L. Crowl) were forgettable examples of bottom-drawer generic horror.* **Nematodes***! (1988) concerns the evil doings of a gang of scientists whose brains have been colonized by mutant worms.* **Blood Mushroom** *(1989) features an inbred family of serial killers cultivating edible fungi on the bodies of their victims.* **Going Bats** *(1991) was a departure, belonging as much to* **vampire romance** *as to horror, although critics objected to her stereotyping of people with mental health issues and found the sex scenes risible.*

(From **Modern Horror Writers,** Random House, 2021)

No one who knew Sallie Crowl had any idea she had once been a writer. That period of her life had been brief, and was so far in the past that she hardly remembered it herself. She thought it best forgotten, along with the unhappy love affairs that had marked her late twenties. After qualifying as a psychiatric nurse she had moved out west and developed new interests. Her job kept her busy, as did volunteer work at the local animal shelter, and in her spare time she preferred to watch old films, read, or follow auctions on eBay rather than waste time making up stories no one else wanted to read. So the email from Spain might have been meant for another person.

Dear S·L· Crowl:

My name is Antonio Cuentas, I am a professional translator, and I write to you on behalf of

11

Libros del Infierno, a small publisher based in Barcelona, to enquire about the possibility of acquiring Catalan and Spanish language rights to your novel Going Bats· Being such a small concern, they can offer only 1,000 Euro as advance payment, but if the book proves popular as they hope, you will receive 17% royalties on sales, plus 50% of digital and other subsidiary rights·

I wish you to know I am personally a big, big fan of your amazing and wonderful book, and brought it to the attention of this publisher, having translated it 'off my own bat' (ha ha)·

If you agree, as I sincerely hope, then I will send you the contract by return, unless you direct me to an agent·

Looking forward to hearing from you very soon·

With warmest regards from Spain,
Antonio

If it was a scam, surely the money offered would be more tempting than 1,000 euros, and she couldn't think of anyone from the past who would have bothered to track her down and tease her like this.

The publisher did exist – at least, it had a website. The Spanish titles meant nothing to her, but she recognized the names Ambrose Bierce and Ramsey Campbell on their list. And they wanted to publish S.L. Crowl!

She was an author again, astonished by how happy that made her.

The contract arrived, in English, and it looked all right, but, just to have a comparison, she went up to the attic to fetch the file box containing all correspondence connected with her three published novels, as well as the manuscripts of the five she had failed to sell.

While there, she found the box of twenty mint copies of *Going Bats.* For a long time, she could not stand to look at these reminders of her failure, but now that stupid cover with its nasty, leering bat made her think of Antonio's email, and she felt a thrill. She had a fan! She was going to be published again! All right, it would be in another country, in languages she could not read – but those were mere details.

Dear Antonio,

I am still curious about how you happened to find my book in the first place. It was never a big seller and has been out of print for two decades, at least.

Dear Sallie,

When I was thirteen, my family spent a month's holiday in the US – mostly New York and Florida. Part of the deal was that we kids would improve our English. I was a shy, retiring boy and did not relish conversations with strangers, always with my nose in a book· So my father told me I could buy any book I liked, so long as it was in English· There was a kind of super-drugstore nearby with a book section, and one paperback in particular attracted me strangely· The image of that monstrous, grinning bat flapping above the head of the cowering girl held a terrible fascination· I knew it would give me nightmares – my father did not approve – but, being a man of honour, he kept his word and let me have it·

Of course, I found it hard to read· So many words! But I was motivated to persevere, determined to master the content of this "unsuitable" adult, potentially terrifying book· I read with the dictionary ever at my side, but even so, sometimes I could only guess at the significance of what I was so laboriously translating, and much of your novel's true meaning_escaped me entirely – but I was hooked· I read it again, many times – until that poor book fell apart·

Later, I found and read the other two novels by S. L. Crowl: entertaining stories, but barely hinting at the masterpiece to come.

My question: Was "Going Bats" really your last book? When I asked you before why you published nothing more, you said 'the horror market had tanked' but with GB you had proved you were more than 'just' a horror writer, and if even a boy like me could see that, surely savvy New York editors would have been duelling for the rights to publish you. So what happened?

Did you adopt a pseudonym for your more literary work? If you trust me with your secret, I promise not to tell. I am more honoured than I can say to have been allowed to be the official translator of GOING BATS into both Spanish and Catalan, and knowing how easy it would have been for you to turn down our meagre financial offer, please believe me that I would never willingly cause you or your American publisher the slightest worry. This is for me alone. Want me to guess? Are you really Joyce Carol Oates?

She had to laugh, otherwise the tears that came to her eyes on reading his charmingly naïve missive would have been too painful.

She wrote back and explained that no one before him had seen such promise in *Going Bats*. It had attracted no particular attention when published; she remembered only two reviews, and the one in *Locus* had been pretty savage. She had acquired an agent after selling her first two novels; he'd taken her to a different publisher and got a slightly bigger advance for *Going Bats*, but after he had failed to sell the next three books, he washed his hands of her. About a year after that, she'd made the decision to stop writing.

You have THREE unpublished novels??

Actually, five.

OMG!!! Like GOING BATS? Or straight horror? Or something else?

More like GOING BATS - stand-alone horror/romance hybrids, if there is such a thing (probably not, which may be why they did not sell!)

You can sell them to Libros del Infierno. I am sure of it. It may not be what you want - and not what you deserve - to be known and have your talent recognized only here, not your own country — but perhaps it could be a beginning to your rediscovery as a major author·

Sallie was dazzled, dizzied, charmed. She thrilled to his emails, full of promises about her glorious future and wonderful novels. Dear Antonio. She felt like a woman in love, although she recognized her emotions were not for the unknown man himself, but rather the future that he set out for her — his promises of recognition, a new readership, and maybe, someday, fame and fortune. And literary respectability. Even her wildest daydreams twenty-five years ago had not gone that far. Then, she had hoped only to make a living from writing, and to have some fans like Antonio.

Dear Antonio. She knew so little about him — he might be gay, married or celibate — but she was old enough to be his mother, and his passion was for her work. And wasn't that the best thing? Even though she had sold three books, they had been of the forgettable, disposable kind, reviewed, if at all, with a superior sneer. If she had fans, she'd never met them. But now, finally, somebody "got" what she had been trying to do, and would champion her book for a whole new nation and generation of readers.

El Murciélago and *Rata Pinyada* — the titles of, respectively, the Spanish and Catalan editions — were to be published on April 23rd. The date was significant as Cervantes' birthday and the feast of Saint George — Sant Jordi, the patron saint of Catalonia. Antonio told her this was the biggest day for book sales in the whole region. Traditionally, men and boys give red roses to their wives, mothers and sweethearts, and are given books in return.

Of course that is a bit sexist now, he said. *So mostly everybody gives books to everybody else —*

*and women still expect to get a rose as well·
You can't beat it for boosting book sales, and
all the publishers and booksellers make the most
of it·*

*The city will be en fete with parties and live
music, bookstalls along the Ramblas, authors
making appearances to sign books and talk with
readers· Too bad our publisher cannot afford to
fly you in, but I will be there to promote our
book, never fear!*

April was still six months away – Sallie had a week of
vacation time. She couldn't really afford it, but the
publisher's advance ought to cover her air fare, and for the
rest, she had a credit card.

When she told Antonio, he was as happy as she could
have hoped, and told her the publishers would supply her
with a hotel room for two nights, and her meals would also
be taken care of. In return, she'd be asked to do a book
signing session, and maybe a few interviews. Antonio
himself would meet her at the airport, and serve as her guide
and interpreter for as long as she needed him. Advance
proofs were now being sent out to reviewers, and everyone
was very excited.

Advance proofs. Reviewers. Book signing. Interviews.
None of these things had featured in her brief career as a
writer. Barcelona shimmered in her mind like a dream of
paradise.

Her first impression of Antonio Cuentas in the flesh was
that he could have been the model for Grey Hartaker, the

hero/villain of *Going Bats*. Tall, with a powerful physique, saturnine features, deep-set penetrating brown eyes and thick dark hair that grew into a pronounced widow's peak – he was almost spookily handsome, and so matched her vision of a romantic vampire that when she first set eyes on him in El Prat Aeorporte, she had to pinch herself to make sure she was not still asleep and dreaming somewhere over the Atlantic.

"Sallie?"

"Antonio?"

He swooped and his lips brushed her right cheek and then her left. "Welcome to Barcelona. Your first time, yes?"

Giddy from his touch, the spicy amber scent of his aftershave, the soft growl of his voice, Sallie could only giggle. As he regarded her quizzically, she gasped, "My first time *anywhere* outside America."

"Then we must make it the most memorable visit of your life. Your bag? Come – the city awaits."

She had flown overnight, and scarcely slept at all, from excitement and the uncomfortable seat, but she felt revitalized and rejuvenated by Antonio's presence as he guided her outside, into the morning sunshine. (*So, not a vampire, then*, she thought, and giggled.)

He gave her a quizzical look. "What's funny?"

"Sorry – it's the excitement."

He smiled. "I know. And for me, too, this publication is very special. I have worked as a professional translator for more than twelve years, but this one was different, not an assignment, but a labour of love. So I have a strong personal stake in its success."

They reached his car, a small red Fiat. "It is still a bit early for checking in to your hotel so, I thought I would show you the city first – if you would like?"

She didn't know what she would like but nodded her eager agreement.

It turned out Antonio meant quite literally to 'show her

the city', for he took her up a mountain, Tibidabo, overlooking Barcelona, and then to the nearby Torre de Collserola, a communications tower designed by an English architect for the 1992 Olympics. A glass elevator whisked them to the thirteenth level where viewing platforms provided a 360° view of the city, the mountains and the sea that bordered it.

The view was spectacular, but she had already been up in the air for hours, and was eager to get back down to earth. When Antonio asked her which of Barcelona's many famous landmarks she would like to visit first, the only one she could think of was Gaudí's still-unfinished church of the Sagrada Familia.

"Of course! But first, I think we will have coffee."

Tourists swarmed the area around Sagrada Familia, and Sallie hated crowds. Even energized by coffee and a pastry, even with her guide so tall and strong by her side, she shrank from the prospect of merging with them or fighting her way through, and he was so sensitive to her change in mood that before she could say it, he suggested they return another time: "Early morning is best, to be ahead of the crowds."

He took her to her hotel, located in the Barri Gòtic, the medieval part of the city, helped her check in, and told her he would come back for her at three, to take her to lunch with their publishers. Sallie thought that seemed very late for lunch, but she was very glad to have time for a nap.

Lunch was substantial – steak and potatoes in an Argentine restaurant. Her publishers were an attractive young married couple called Josep and Carolina, and they seemed oddly nervous, continually apologizing for not having been able to pay her airfare, thanking her for coming, and paying her lavish compliments about her book, which they felt deeply honoured to have been allowed to publish. It took a while, but gradually the realization dawned: they were in awe of her. As if she really were somebody like Joyce Carol Oates, a literary genius and best-seller in America, and not a forgotten, over-the-hill genre writer.

I could get used to this, she thought, exchanging an amused glance with Antonio (who once again seemed able to read her mind), and did her best to put Josep and Carolina at their ease, while resisting the tug towards a proud pomposity.

They presented her with copies of *La Murciélago* (Spanish) and *Rata Pinyada* (Catalan) – beautiful books; although both were paperbacks, the difference between the European books, in size, paper quality, binding, and appearance, and the American paperback original, was extreme. The cover was elegant, a suggestive, not lurid, work of Gothic art.

They all toasted the book's success. Wine flowed, and it was delicious, better than any she had tasted before. For once, Sallie did not hold back or refuse refills. She wasn't paying, and she didn't have to drive, or do anything but stagger back to her hotel and sink into blissful sleep.

But over coffee she learned that there was a dinner party scheduled for later – a large event hosted by a bookstore chain. "I don't think I could possibly eat anything more," she said, dismayed, glancing at her watch to see that it was already five-thirty.

"Don't worry about that," said Antonio. "We eat very late in Barcelona."

Next morning, she woke in a big, beautiful bed in a big, beautiful hotel room, sunshine streaming through the curtains, happy and rested yet still full of the exhilaration of the celebrations of the night before. More wine – more people – more incomprehensible conversations (although Antonio, bless him, had kept his promise and stayed beside her, ready to murmur translations into her ear, she mostly let it wash over her, shaking hands and air-kissing strange faces and smiling, always smiling) – more indulging in the feeling of being a minor celebrity. She might as well enjoy it while it lasted.

Today was book day, *el dia de llibre,* San Jordi, and Antonio would be picking her up downstairs in – oh, goodness, half an hour! It would take her that long just to do her face and hair...

In the lobby, Antonio presented her with a single red rose.

"No book?" She was afraid she was blushing, and hoped it was not obvious how personally she took this traditional gift.

"Well, do you have one for me?"

"I brought you the manuscript of the best one of my unpublished novels – does that count?"

"The best gift I could ever imagine," he assured her, eyes flaring with pleasure. "But where is it? I don't see anything like that in your hands, and your bag is too small."

"It's up in my room – but you don't want to carry it around all day."

He seemed to struggle against temptation before conceding: "Yes, better I should get it later. Why only one? You know I want to read them all."

His eagerness was balm after the rejections in the past. "One step at a time. You don't even know if they'll want another book – we don't know if this one will sell."

"Josep and Carolina are certain of it, and they know their business. You should trust them. I do."

"I trust you," she said with excessive warmth.

Her first book-signing. She was one of five authors, seated at separate tables at the back of a huge, well-stocked bookshop. Sallie was the only foreign author. Two of the book-signers were clearly popular, attracting long lines of patient customers, and the room was filled with the happy buzz of excited conversation. People who came up to Sallie were more reserved, perhaps shy about trying to communicate with someone who did not speak their language. Sallie sympathized, grateful for Antonio's constant, vigilant presence. She signed about a dozen books, with no idea if that meant success or disappointment to the bookshop owners. She was impressed that so many strangers were willing to take a chance on an unknown author and spend 20 euros on a paperback – no matter how beautifully produced.

The session was nearly over when a grey-haired bearded man rushed up to Sallie's table and introduced himself in English – he said he was a publisher from Paris. "I read your book last night, Miss Crowl, and I honestly could not put it down. I could not sleep for reading it. It is simply wonderful. Like nothing I have read before. I must publish it. Your Spanish publisher says there is no agent – you handle all rights yourself, is that correct?"

"Well, yes, at the moment." Taken by surprise, she glanced at Antonio, who, alert to her unspoken question as ever, gave a response:

"Miss Crowl is currently considering her publisher's offer to handle all non-English language rights on her behalf."

Sallie could not remember when Josep or Carolina had said anything about this – but so much had been said at the noisy, festive lunch and ridiculously late supper yesterday that she had been driven to smile and nod her agreement to almost everything, whether she heard it or not. And so, trusting Antonio, she smiled and nodded now. "That's right," she told the French publisher. "I will tell Josep and Carolina to get in touch with you after we have, you know, signed an agreement, and I am sure we will."

"Oh, good," he said, not looking happy. "Well, please remind them that I was the first to express an interest, and will make it a formal offer as soon as they like." He took a breath. "In the meantime, I would very much like to read your original novel. It seems rather difficult to find in the usual places on the internet."

"Oh, that's no problem. Give me your address, and

when I get home I'll send you a copy."

"You are so kind! That would be wonderful," he breathed, gazing into her eyes. "Here, the address is on my card – and my email – perhaps it would be simpler for you to send me the file?"

She almost laughed. "It's from 1990. Remember floppy discs?"

"But you still have extra copies of the book? One you can spare for me?"

"Oh, yes. It's no problem."

He kissed her hand. In America, she would have found it creepy, but here it made her shiver with pleasure as a wonderful, courtly gesture.

Antonio wore a grim expression, and as soon as the other man had left, he tore his card into tiny fragments. Her heart beat faster. Was he *jealous?*

"You must not send him your book." His eyes burned into hers.

"Why not?"

"He is not your publisher – he is only trying to steal a march on all the others – yes, others will want it, and only the best offer will secure it. He knows that."

She blinked rapidly. "You mean, .I should wait until he's made an offer, to let him read it?"

"He has read it." Antonio patted one of the Spanish copies.

"But – the original. I really don't mind, you know – I have plenty –"

"They won't last long if you send them out indiscriminately. Wait – at least until we have a firm deal with a French publisher. Then – well, it is up to you, but, for another reason, I hope you would not." He tilted his head and looked down, as if embarrassed.

"What reason?"

"There are not many copies of *Going Bats* available. It is very hard to find. Yours may be the only ones left, and if you give one away to the French publisher..." He shrugged and opened his hands.

Sallie did not understand. "If I don't, they won't be able to translate it."

"No. So they would have to hire me." Hand on his heart, he looked at her sadly. "But perhaps you would prefer to have a different translator."

She felt her cheeks burning again. "You can translate into French?"

"*Certainment.* Spanish, Catalan, French, Italian and English are my main languages. Of course, the French being what they are, they would never hire a Spaniard to translate a book into their precious language. But, with your agreement, of course, when Josep and Catalina sell the rights, it could be with the proviso of your preferred translator."

It was a career move – of course he would be looking after his own interests, wanting more work, she told herself.

"Sallie, I hope you do not think this is wrong of me. It is your decision, of course, and only yours. But your book is so dear to me. To give it up... to allow someone else to work on it – it makes me shudder to think. This book means more to me than it possibly could to anyone else, certainly to someone for whom it was merely a job done for hire."

It was a declaration of love. True, it was for her writing, not herself, but the line between book and author is a narrow one. She melted before his passion, unable to refuse.

The rest of the day passed in a blur. She was introduced to too many people to recall; looked at books she could not read; gave an interview; wandered through the warm, vibrant city with Antonio at her side; ate a large meal of excellent food late in the afternoon, part of a convivial crowd of strangers who seemed, after a few more glasses of the delicious wine, like her best friends. Finally, around ten o'clock that night, she was in a bar with Antonio and other people she could not exactly remember. A plate of cold meats and cheese was ordered for the table, and someone brought bread and olives.

"Will this be enough? Would you rather go out for a meal?" Antonio asked her.

"Oh, this is great, thank you." She reached for a thin slice of ham.

"Miss Crowl?"

A young man with a round face, glasses, curly brown hair, a red scarf wrapped around his neck, enveloped in a khaki jacket that seemed too warmly padded for the mild spring weather, looked down at her, holding a copy of *El Murciélago*. "I am right, you are Miss Crowl the authoress?"

"I am Sallie Crowl the *author*."

He continued to smile at her but said nothing, so she asked, "Did you want me to sign your book?"

He shook his head. "I want you to know that I know."

"Know what?"

His smile turned malicious. "You're busted. I'm a book blogger. This one, I was sent an advance copy for review. I was very impressed. A magnificent work, I thought. Most unusual mix of horror and humanity. One for grown-up readers, an ironic commentary on all those ridiculous vampire love romances that teenage girls adore, while at the same time very... very sensitive, very subtle. Also, disturbing. Psychologically very strong."

"Thank you," she said uneasily.

"Yet, something bothered me. The English title – *Going Bats*. It was familiar, but I could find nothing about it on the internet. Not a prize winner, never reviewed? I began to feel I had read it in my youth. So I went back to my parents' house, and it was there, although when I held it in my hand, nothing came back to me. Perhaps, I thought I had been too young to appreciate the subtle nuance of your style, or the language had defeated me.

"I have no problem *now* to read in English, so yesterday, I read your book. This one." He reached inside his bulky jacket and withdrew the familiar American paperback with its monstrous, leering bat. "*This* is a horror, nothing more. Not even a good horror! A pretence at romance – sickening

– and stupid violence – no awareness of real human nature – absurd, grotesque."

Sallie was bewildered. The guy was angry, but what had she done? That was certainly her book that he kept brandishing, like a preacher with a cross, but what did he mean? First he loves it, then he hates it – how was that her fault?

She turned, of course, to Antonio, and found he was already on his feet.

"Who's this?" asked the man. "Your husband?"

"Antonio Cuentas, my translator."

Eyes widened, then narrowed. "*Translator?* Are the publishers in on it?"

"What do you mean?" asked Sallie. "What does he mean?"

"We're leaving," said Antonio, a hand on her back, steering her firmly across the room.

The guy followed them outside. "Don't walk away from me. Even if you won't talk, I will write about it anyway. I don't know what's going on, but this is not right, you're covering something up, and you're not getting away with it. I'll make sure everyone knows. I have my proof, right here. Unless, of course, you have a good explanation. You had better tell me your story."

Helpless to stop against Antonio's determined forward movement, Sallie could only cast a backward glance, and the shadows cast by the yellow streetlamps made it hard to read his expression. "What story? I don't know what you're talking about."

"No? You wish for me to spell it out?"

Antonio stopped abruptly, turned around, and said something in rapid Spanish. The other man replied the same way, and for the next minute or two Sallie could only stand and watch without understanding. Even the purpose of this conversation was obscure to her: were they in opposition, or was it a misunderstanding, to be explained away?

Some sort of agreement was reached. Antonio told

Sallie, "We are going somewhere more private than that other bar, to talk quietly."

"And you will answer my questions, Miss Crowl."

She nodded up at Antonio, trusting that he knew what he was doing.

Their relative positions had changed without her wanting it. Now Antonio and the stranger walked side by side, and Sallie followed. She picked up her pace, wanting to be close to her translator as before, but his stance repelled her approach. He didn't want her there. Sick at heart, she took the hint and fell back.

The men were walking more quickly now through the nearly deserted streets of the Barri Gòtico, and Sallie had to struggle to keep them in view. Having been led around by Antonio since she'd arrived, she had very little sense of where anything was in this confusing city, and she was afraid of getting lost.

They took another sharp turn and were out of sight. Sallie almost ran to catch up, and as she rounded the corner she saw something happen between them, but could not understand it. Did the guy slip on something, or stumble? It seemed like Antonio was trying to help him, but there was something odd.

Heart pounding hard, Sallie stood still and stared. She saw the stranger fall against one of the old stone buildings that lined the street. There was no noise, no cry of pain, but presumably he'd hit his head, because next he was sliding down the wall until he was sprawled, half sitting, back supported by the wall, head drooping, like a discarded doll.

Antonio bent over the man – checking his pulse, or his breathing? But he was going inside the bulky jacket – to feel for a heartbeat?

When he straightened up and turned to face Sallie, he had the copy of *Going Bats* in his hand.

"What happened?" Her voice sounded strange to herself, too high and squeaky.

Antonio looked unruffled. He wasn't even breathing

hard. He took Sallie's arm and led her back in the direction she had come. "*Estaba borracho.*"

"What?"

"Drunk. Or maybe drugs."

"No! He didn't seem –"

"Yes he did. It was obvious – maybe more obvious to me."

"But – should we leave him?" They had already left, and were leaving him further behind with every step.

Antonio snorted. "You want to go back and stay by that imbecile, watch over him through the night? Someone will find him."

"The police?"

"You leave that to me. If the police want to question you – which is very unlikely – I will tell you what to say."

Her stomach dropped, as if she'd stepped over the edge of a cliff. She looked at Antonio's other hand, but the paperback had disappeared. She swallowed hard. "What –"

"I'll tell you what to say," he repeated. "Stick to my story, and everything will work out fine."

*Crowl's break-out novel of 2017 (actually first published in Spanish by Libros del Infierno as **El Murciélago**, 2016) – **My Man Bat** – echoes and refracts the basic premise of **Going Bats,** but could never be mistaken for the crude generic horror/romance of that apprentice work. Her new style glittered with a literary assurance and psychological acuity that astonished the critics and won for her the Shirley Jackson Award and the World Fantasy Award, as well as a spot on the New York Times best-seller list. Made into the film of the same name (DreamWorks, 2019), and with translation rights sold in more than twenty countries, it marked an unexpected new beginning to a successful and prolific writing career which has so far seen three more novels, beginning with....*

(From **Modern Horror Writers,** 2021, Random House)

Secret Stories of Doors

Sofia Rhei

Para Chús Arellano

The controversy around Sor Assumpció's work is, indeed, one of the most interesting cases of the XVIII century regarding the soft apology of Satanism. The reasons given by her advocates were that the book followed the perfect pattern of a cautionary tale, giving the right advice at every moment, and punishing the characters when they did make a bad choice, even if the possibility of a Christian redemption was always left open. The attacks were centred of the portrait of the friendly and charming figure of evil, arguing that such a fascinating and warm personality would attract, rather than repel, young or suggestible readers.

Leopoldo de Manresa
The Borders Between Faith and Heresy in the Inquisition Times,
Salamanca, 1907.

Joan Perucho had spent the night working, bent over his bench at home. He lived in a microscopic apartment in the Gracia district, and most of the cupboards were filled with writing machines, artisan presses and homemade contraptions such as the paper eroder or the gelatine photocopier. He was creating happily, humming a tune, and barely noticing the lack of sleep.

"Most of the works of the Benedictine sister were hidden by the chief nun when the inquisition began the investigation. Some of the theatre plays were lost forever. Fortunately, the cautionary tales were already in circulation, though they became a risky business for the printer. He continued selling *Secret Stories of Doors* under the counter, accepting the risk of prosecution if caught."

Leopoldo Galván,
Cursed Poets in the Spanish Church, Valladolid, 1929.

The alarm clock startled him. He had forgotten about it, absorbed in the process of dying a false newspaper page with black tea, to make it look older.

Fire at the school in Sant Pere mes Baix Street.

Although the fire was rapidly controlled, two firemen lost their lives fighting the flames. The fire was caused by a coal brazier the doorman didn't extinguish properly. One wall caught light, revealing that it was made of wood; behind it, the firemen found several hidden books and documents, probably banned during the Inquisition years. One of them was a cautionary tale by Sor Assumpció Ardebol, which scholars believed to be lost forever. The reparations will take a week, during which time there will be no classes at the school; parents are advised to keep their children at home and await instructions.

La Vanguardia, Barcelona, April 17th 1949

He looked at the documents he had created, and smiled, satisfied. This entry in the Encyclopaedia would be one of his biggest personal triumphs. As one of the millions of workers for the Barcelona-based World Encyclopaedia, with their ink-proof dark uniforms, he would have found daily life unbearable without his game of introducing invented information into the general database. At the beginning, they were just details: a small quote, a fabricated minor character, a picturesque anecdote of a well-known public figure. Over the years, he had managed to introduce more significant apocrypha, giving birth to full, juicy fruit, and even branches and trees of misinformation.

He never kept a record of the fictions. That would be too dangerous, because the aerial police could spy on homes at any moment since the 1969 curtain ban. Joan hid the machines in the white cupboards, and got ready to work.

He was about to exit the apartment when a thin serpent, made of green paper, slithered under his door:

Don't go to work. Instead, go to Carrer de n'Arai.

Joan felt his pulse accelerate. For years, especially since his 'alterations' of documental history had escalated, he had been afraid of being discovered. He crushed the serpent in his hand and put it under the water tap to dissolve.

He had heard about this kind of message. There was nothing specific written on it, no accusation or even mention of his illicit tinkering. He had heard about traps made by the aerial police: when someone was considered a suspect but there was no way to prove he had transgressed. Avoiding work and visiting a suspect place, one of the escape enclaves of the outsiders, would provide proof enough of his guilt.

No, he must not alter his daily routine. He became calmer after reaching that decision. He had been careful, *very* careful, with the destruction of the fake documents he had generated and scanned. And, as he liked to repeat inside his head, as a leitmotif of his falsification-devoted life, it was very hard to prove that something once reported had not actually happened. Especially when most of the historical archives and newspaper libraries were located outside of town, sometimes as far as Huesca or Castellón. Perucho used to enjoy those trips, particularly the silence. Aerial police were so abundant in the city that the humming helixes were a permanent noise/feature, like a roaring, metallic sea.

Perucho took a look through the window, but no one was there. No flying policeman was observing him from the other side of the regulation-sized clear window. But it felt as if they were always there. The threat of their appearance was almost as daunting as the appearance itself.

Perucho took a deep breath. He had been very careful. He always made sure not to stand out for any reason, not overproducing or under. He studied the statistics and ensured that his productivity matched that of his peers. And, as most of his supervisors did not even understand Spanish or Catalan, he usually generated the false documents in one of those languages.

Of course there were rumours of people being led away

by the police and never returning, though Perucho had never seen it happen. In fact, there were no specific rules about being strictly 'accurate' and not being a little inventive. Everything was kind of vague and generic, leaving room for a certain lax interpretation of the regulations.

But the main reason for Perucho to ignore the warning and go to work as usual was his deep desire to do so. The project about the fictional Sor Assumpció Ardebol and her non-existent *Secret Stories of Doors* was perhaps his best creations to date. These projects were his reason to live, the only possible free literary writing in a world where fiction was only allowed in commercial and sanctioned forms: indoctrination, role-model creation and such.

Most days, Perucho walked from home to work, and he didn't want to make an exception today. He tried not to walk faster or slower than normal, and to keep to all his daily routines, such as stopping by the bakery to buy a small butifarra-filled roll for lunch.

Ten years before, the Global Government had decided to assign specific functions to several strategically placed cities. Barcelona was chosen to become the Capital of Knowledge. The World Encyclopaedia had been based there since the forties, so it was just a matter of increasing the space and personnel assigned to the task of gathering verifiable data, deciding what was important and what wasn't worth a mention, and classifying it all.

Barcelona had always been a multicultural city, but the arrival of millions of Fundamental Knowledge System employees from all around the globe, in order to cover all the possible languages and dialects both alive and dead, had turned the city into a new, improved Babel.

All the central patios of the blocks in the Ensanche had been *upgraded*, according to the official term, to host twenty-five storey buildings. All of them were identical, and identically filled with the Encyclopaedia workers. The lower levels were full of presses and printers, and technical workers wearing black, ink-proof uniforms. The upper floors, such as the one where Joan Perucho worked, were provided with a linotype machine for each of the editors. These were dressed in anthracite suits: even if they didn't work with ink, and were not at risk of staining themselves, they had to wear a dark colour, as if knowledge might also leave a permanent and disgusting stain.

Fear came suddenly, in the form of paranoid thoughts: what if there were an undisclosed control system, a secret body of agents devoted to pursuing the truth and punishing the introducers of false data, determined to send them to humid and squalid prisons which they would never leave again?

Joan Perucho entered the building with his usual smile, repeating to himself the mantra: *it is almost impossible to prove that something has not happened.* In fact, were he tasked to find proof that some book, review or article had *not* been published it would take him months. He had never heard of such a commission, and he seriously doubted the Fundamental Knowledge System would use paid work hours to distinguish between documental truth and lies. There was no need to; most of the employees were predictable conformists, bootlickers, as grey as their suits.

As he entered the packed elevator, he felt cold sweat trickle down his nape and tried to calm himself. He went to his linotype, in the Catalan section, casually took out the fake documents, and dispersed them between dozens of genuine ones. And, as every day, he began to type.

The morning passed without incident. Joan took heart and accelerated the typing of false documents. He had lunch in the workplace and continued introducing spurious lines and lines:

Sor Assumpció Ardebol depicts the darkest streets of old Barcelona under the form of a descent to hell, both literal and metaphorically. El Raval is unknown and risky, a foreing land for decent people, but also the place were a truly satanic encounter can occurr. The true risk are not the thieves, drug-addict beggars

or crazy vagabonds, but the "small doors", inadvertent thresholds, often concealed by shadows.
Juana Torregrosa, *Images of Barcelona*, Barcelona, 1955.

"Perucho" said a monotone, dispassionate voice, "the boss wants to see you in his office. At five."

Perucho tried to control his shaking hands. He was not often called to the director's desk, but it happened sometimes. Maybe this was just for routine verifications: "Perucho, how is the work going?" "Very well, sir." "Have you found enough materials to maintain you daily quote of entries?" "Yes, sir." "Would you need another documental trip to Girona?" "Maybe next month, sir."

The temptation to escape, to run out with some slight excuse, was almost overwhelming. But Joan Perucho had a strong mind. He inhaled deeply, discretely, and told himself an old joke:

A Catalan was in front of a fishbowl with only a fish in it. Amazingly, when the man looked up, the fish seemed to copy him and went in the same direction. The same thing happened when the man looked in other directions.

A Spaniard, watching the catalan, went to talk to him.

"¡This is incredible! ¡Marvelous!"said the Spaniard. "¿How can you make the fish follow your command?"

"It is very easy," the Catalan answered calmly. "I stare deeply to the eyes of the animal to subject it to my will. The inferior fish mind acknowledges the superior human mind. With a little practice, I'm sure you can get the same result in no time."

This seemed entirely reasonable to the Spaniard. After all, he had never tried to command a fish before. Surely, it was a piece of cake. He began to stare the fish deep in the eye.

Ten minutes later, the Catalan man returned to the fishbowl.

"¿How is it going?" he asked the Spaniard.

The Spaniard turned with a vacant look, his lips pursed in the form of a fish mouth.

"¡Blub! ¡Blub! ¡Blub!" he gaped.

Perucho laughed to himself. No matter how many times

he had heard or told the joke, it was still his favourite and never failed to cheer him up. He looked at the big clock on the wall, and saw it was almost four. He had a full hour to work: if he was going to get caught, he had better finished the project first.

"Some letters?" asked the girl with the trolley, offering him small baskets of metallic vowels and consonants.

"Some "F's" and "V's", please" answered Perucho.

"*¡El bombín! ¡Ha vingut el bombín!*", one of the editors whispered in Catalan, as a warning.

El bombín was one of the senior leaders, the boss of the boss of their boss, if Perucho had gotten it right. He was rarely seen in the office, and when he was, he liked to find fault with the workers. "Sit properly, Balagué!", or "this is not the right way to position your hands over the keyboard, Fontanella. I hope you don't expect the Fundamental Knowledge System Foundation to pay for the medical expenses you will get if you insist on not correcting your posture."

All the editors tensed instantly. Joan Perucho didn't. He was already in a perfect position, as was his habit. He had learnt to maintain his spine in a vertical position to avoid back pains and fatigue. Maybe that was the reason *el bombín* had never made an observation about him. Sometimes Perucho was under the impression that *el bombín* had a very peculiar sense of humour and that he just enjoyed startling the workers.

But instead of his usual round through the linotypists, *el bombín* went right to the boss' office, and closed the door after him. The workers relaxed automatically, with the exception of Perucho. He needed three more internal jokes and a little bit of silent meditation to regain his composure.

He typed a last article entitled "The portrait of the devil in Sor Assumpció Ardebol's work." It was his favourite, the pearl in the crown of the fictional author he had invented. In the article, an equally fictional PHD candidate explained that in the nun's cautionary tales, the devil was always depicted as a person with their right ear missing. The meaning of this characterization would be a metaphor for the people who only want to hear the bad half of the words, the wrong side of every story, and so had a negative perception about human nature.

When the article was done, Perucho took the letter tray, perfectly composed, put it in the plate elevator, and sent it to the printing machine. When that was done, his whole body relaxed. Now his last work would be part of the Encyclopaedia irretrievably. He could be arrested now. He almost welcomed it.

But *el bombín* was still with the boss half an hour later, and then an hour, and then two. At seven, the anthracite editors began to abandon their workplaces. Perucho worked for an additional half an hour, which was not unusual for him, waiting for *el bombín* to leave. But it didn't happen.

"Casals," he said to the boss' secretary, "Mister Coole asked me to come and see him some hours ago."

"Don't worry about it, Perucho. He is still with *el*... with mister Gladstone. I suspect they'll be a while."

"Are you sure? Because I can wait..."

Casals smiled.

"You are too conscientious. Just go home, the boss will still be here tomorrow."

Perucho thanked her and left, light of leg and even lighter of mind.

He had been right all along: there was nothing to worry about. If something were wrong, Casals would know for sure; the boss couldn't find his own shadow without his hyper-efficient secretary. And she was as nice and friendly as she had always been.

He left the building in a state of relieved euphoria. He even whistled a bit. Manipulating information to create his personal world gave him a wonderful thrill: a spark in the darkness, a colour splash in the grey reality that the world had become after the global disasters at the end of the fifties.

An aerial agent passed by Perucho and sniffed at him. The boots of the agent almost touched Perucho's shoulder. However, the presence didn't feel threatening but reassuring. Things were in order again.

He could go to the nocturnal thrift market, los Encantes, and find some ancient books to read just for pleasure. Or return to his apartment and begin his next project. Something about spas... some ideas had been bugging him, bubbling away in his mind as if it was the very hot tub he wanted to talk about.

Yes, he should be doing one of those things. Why then was he walking in the direction suggested that morning by the paper serpent? *Carer de n'Arai.* Why had he memorised it?

He should avoid problems. Going to the place specified by the message would be madness. What if the message wasn't just a joke, or a random bureaucratic trap? What if someone really knew about his infractions? And, even scarier, what if these unknown friends really wanted to help him avoid certain punishment?

But he couldn't help himself. He was doomed, trapped by his own curiosity, and so walked down to Portaferrissa with a frozen smile of dissimulation. Oddly, he was more afraid in the open street than he had been at the office. Maybe the work space, so familiar, had provided reassurance.

There was no one in the street. When Perucho was younger, Barcelona had been a vibrant city. He remembered the cinema Les Delícies, with its crowd of kids, workers and grandpas; he remembered going to Tibidabo and its spooky museum of automatons, or to Parc de la Ciutadella with its spectacular greenhouse. But that city was lost forever. The bombs had fallen in a thick rain, devastating blocks and even whole quarters, erasing a world, an entire époque.

He was almost in Portaferrissa. And then, at the corner, he saw an archer. Partially hidden in shadow, the woman, dressed in the official uniform of an urban cleaner, was tensing her arm, an arrow pointing at a cat. She looked stressed.

"I don't know what to do" she said. "It's trapped on the roof, meowing constantly. A cat without an owner is a menace to hygiene, a potential pest carrier, and we have already received a complaint from the neighbours. On the other hand... He looks so confused. But I can't reach him from the ground. Maybe if I could the poor animal might have a chance... The zoo...? Or I could get fired for not killing it."

Perucho felt something tickle his nose, like static or the presence of an intruding insect. It was the taste of the unexpected, of the marvellous. It was so rare, and mixed deliciously with the feeling of fear.

Curiosity killed the cat, Perucho thought immediately, or *qui escolta pels forats, sent els seus pecats* in Catalan: he who pokes around in inappropriate places perceives his own sins. In both cases, the wrong, the *devil*, lay in the thirst for the new, for information, knowledge. The archer looked like a personification, or even a *prosopopoeia*, as the ancients might have said, of curiosity herself.

"Maybe you can fire an arrow at the wall, just there, you see? Maybe the cat could use that as a step and get down by himself... Then you could catch it."

And then he added, in a whisper.

"Or not."

The woman looked at him.

"You don't want me to kill the cat?"

Perucho had a moment of doubt. A normal citizen would have supported killing the cat, or even threatened the cleaning agent for not fulfilling her duty.

Instead, he said: "No."

"Are you sure?"

"No one needs to die in the name of words."

The archer smiled and then took away her hat, revealing she had no right ear, exactly like the demon in the works of Sor Assumpció Ardebol. She look at him intently. Perucho felt a shiver.

"Will you come with me?" the archer asked.

"Yes."

At this point, he had a sense of being inside one of his own stories that outweighed his fear.

Perucho followed his guide through narrow streets, and arrived in front of another door, almost invisible among the shadows. He entered the building and, on seeing what was inside, couldn't believe his eyes.

He saw a fully functioning old fashioned press, hosting every kind of printing device since printing began. Several people were making artisanal papers. There was even a copyist monk, called la Moreneta: a monastic scribe alive and well in 1975.

It was, obviously, a clandestine workshop. The windows were small and translucent, and the walls were designed to absorb any noise. Only in El Raval could a place like this could remain hidden. The shadows wrapping all the quarter were simultaneously a warning and a protection.

And then Perucho saw *el bombín*. He was walking amongst the industrious workers, and his attitude was very different to the one Perucho was used to. Instead of looking for irregularities and tiny faults, he seemed relaxed. Even happy. He looked like a completely different person.

"¡Ah! Perucho, so glad to see you!" he said in Catalan. Perucho hadn't realised *el bombín* was fluent in the traditional language. "¡Come, come here! There is nothing you need to worry about. Just enjoy watching the amazing crafts of all these artisans, as I do. You will not have much time to relax, since our team of writers are keen to ask you questions..."

"¿Is this *him*?" asked a woman with glasses, dressed in an inusual shade of green.

"¡Yes! Let me introduce you: Joan Perucho, this is Rosa Fabregat, one of our most brilliant writers."

"Writer..."

Perucho savoured the taste of the word in his mouth. It

was a long time since he had heard it, not to mention pronounced it himself. He felt envious of the young woman.

"Mister Perucho" she said in Catalan, "I am a big admirer of your work."

Perucho was having difficulty processing events.

"But I don't have any 'work'... I'm just one of the editors of the..."

El bombín and Rosa smiled.

"You are an amazing creator. You have built entire literary careers, and even provided most of their works. Octavi de Romeu, Pere Serra y Postius and his monster Bernabó..."

Perucho felt a shiver of fear course down his spine. The woman was talking about his fictional characters as if they were beloved writers. As if they had really existed outside his imagination.

"... by the way, I have a question about Bernabó. We know that he has black fur, no mouth and three eyes. But when he spies the writer, does he focus all the eyes on him or do they have independent movement?"

"Give Perucho a break, my dear Rosa..."

"No, no..." said Perucho. "I've never thought about Bernabó's eyes! It is a beautiful question. Maybe he needs each eye to see a different part of reality – he needs one to see the light and the colour yellow and white, another for the shadows, the blues and greens, and the third for passions, red, purple, pink, magenta. Does this make sense?"

"Then he needs to focus all three eyes on one point at a time… Thank you so much, Mister Perucho."

"You will doubtless get more from him later, Rosa. But for now, he just needs to absorb the place."

"Okay," said she, a little bit frustrated. "Only one more thing... That study about mirrors was... simply perfect"

And she left, failing to see how Perucho blushed.

"She's right. And the medieval stories... they're memorable" continued *el bombín*. Perucho was immensely flattered that this man had spent so much time studying him.

"Manuel," and *el bombín* pointed to one of the artists working over a bench, "is working of that codex you profusely described last year."

"I... I don't understand. Are you creating false documents following the indications I... I made up? Full ones?"

"That is exactly what we are doing. Amazing, isn't it? You will never get caught as a delinquent because the supposedly fake references you have introduced will actually *exist*. Therefore, your work will prove to be factual."

"I need to sit down," said Perucho.

El bombín and Perucho remained silent for a while after Rosa had departed.

"She is in charge of the most delicate and poetic books. A passionate reader, and so full of curiosity for life..."

"But... but why all this effort just to save me... All this must have cost a fabulous amount of..."

"Just to save you? No. To save literature itself, Perucho. You are not the only one 'spicing up' the Encyclopaedia, even if, may I add, you are one of the best. Some of your other colleagues, whom you will meet, such as our beloved Mister Cunqueiro, and Marcel Aymé, who is one of the supervisors of the French language area... Others develop their creational worlds in academia, such as the famous Professor..."

"Torrente Ballester!" Perucho interrupted. "I've always had suspicion about his fonts. Some of his themes are too beautiful to be true."

El bombín sighed.

"As if beauty had to be forcibly different from truth... I'm afraid such are the times we find ourselves in."

"*Estos bueyes tenemos y con ellos tenemos que arar.*"

There was a long silence.

"Perucho," *el bombín* said, "the story of the last decades was not exactly as they... as *we*... have officially been told. The powers that be have made their own 'not exactly true' additions to the Encyclopaedia; not as delightful as yours, I should add. As a well-read man, may I assume you are familiar with the name Herbert George Wells?"

Perucho was surprised. He was expecting great revelations about politics, economics...

"Yes, he was an English writer."

"What if I were to tell you that he shaped the world as we know it?"

"Well... I'd be very surprised"

"In 1935 he wrote a novel..."

The word *novel* sounded so beautiful to Perucho. It contained all the freedom and power from the past art.

"*The Shape of Things to Come,*" *el bombín* continued. "It was a cautionary tale, but not of the classic sort that provides advice for merely the individual. No, this story was about a whole society, and depicted a dark future, the consequence of misguided group behaviour. The book was moderately successful, but in general was considered an extravagant experiment. Why would a serious writer waste his time depicting hypothetical futures?"

Perucho smiled. That kind of book sounded very appealing to him, but maybe he was not the typical reader.

"Three years later, a man called Orson Welles made a radio broadcast. He loved the work of this writer with a similar surname to his, and planned a practical joke for Halloween. He was a perfectionist, so he enlisted colleagues in different radio stations in Britain, Europe and even Russia to create the maximum impact. He wanted to demonstrate to his bosses the immense power of the radio."

"But Todos los Santos, 1938... That was the day of the *coup d'etat* in the old US and Britain..." Perucho interrupted.

"Exactly. Except that in the beginning there was no putsch, just a fake radio transmission about one."

Perucho felt overwhelmed.

"This doesn't make any sense. The overthrow of the government was real. It had far-reaching consequences..."

"After the radio show, people were scared. Many abandoned the cities. Chaos reigned everywhere. The point was proven: radio had power. But at the moment Orson Welles wanted to explain to the world that it had all been just a practical joke, communications were cut everywhere. One of the radical political parties had seized the opportunity and performed a real *coup d'etat.*"

"No one knew what to do. Within a few hours, hastily arranged clandestine meetings took place. Soon, rich oligarchies realised that the new order was far more convenient for them. And the ambitious new leaders arrested Orson Welles. He gave them the book he had drawn inspiration from."

"Are you telling me the shape of the world came from a novel and a radio show?"

"It wasn't that simple. Many agents and interests were involved. But yes, in the end, they thought H. G. Wells' plans were ideal. Why bother to design a new way forward when one had already been mapped out?"

"But you told me Wells' novel was a cautionary tale, not a social proposal..."

"They took it as a handbook. And it worked. They made both Wells and Welles work for them during the early years, and then set them free as reward for their 'cooperation'."

"Forced cooperation..."

El bombín nodded.

"Let me get this straight" said Perucho. "Are you telling me that a fable and a joke gave rise to this economic system, to our whole society? The same society that has banned fiction itself?"

"They limit new creations precisely because they know the impact stories can have."

"Orson Welles was the creator of the regime's propaganda machines for many years, and he did an amazingly good job under several pen names, such as Kane. Nobody knows what he did after that, maybe he just spent the rest of his life on an island, smoking cigars and fathering children. But do we know what H. G. Wells did. He became an entrepreneur and made big money. After all, he knew all the internal mechanisms of power. And with the help of his friend G. K. Chesterton he built a secret institution destined to protect the creators who, like yourself, my dear Perucho, find a way to continue writing fiction in the most adverse of conditions."

Perucho glanced at the machines, this big workshop dedicated to falsification.

"All this came from Wells' funds?" he said, assimilating the new information.

They stood in silence while Perucho observed the ancient 'tórculos', the amanuensis, the papersmiths. He had so many questions... But he was so overwhelmed by the situation that he needed a moment to order his thoughts.

"I need to go for a walk" he said.

El bombín nodded, and gave him the keys of the secret door.

"You can return whenever you wish."

Perucho walked for a long time. The whole city looked different, more intriguing and seductive once he knew the secret Barcelona was hiding. If one clandestine enterprise was working beneath the visible, how many other amazing projects could be living in the shadows?

He arrived to Les Encants, and looked among the piles of old books, abandoned and rejected by so many hands before, lying between used clothes and old crocks, and he bought three of them. He could never resist.

The following day, he went to work as usual.

And the next one, too.

The routine slowly regained its familiar rhythm. And then, on the Thursday, *el bombín* came by his work place.

"Perucho," he said, angrily, "this box is not aligned with the margins. Begin again."

The editor looked at him, astonished. The man was the best actor he had ever seen.

"Yes, sir."

That same afternoon, Perucho returned to the narrow

streets and found the secret door. He opened it with his key. He found Rosa there, who was very happy to see him.

"And now... What? What can I expect? Will my life... change?"

Rosa smiled.

"Not necessarily. We have discovered, through the years, that the simplest way to pursue undercover writing is to do exactly as you are doing: not have any cover at all."

"Then... after all this... I am supposed to go to work tomorrow like any other day, as if this never happened?"

"Yes. Exactly as if this place, all these amazing machines and creators, and our little conversation, were nothing more than... a work of fiction."

Catacomb Saints

Dave Hutchinson

The opening ceremony was in its tenth hour – and the parade of nations was barely halfway completed – when Tomás said, "Why are we watching this rubbish?"

"I'm not watching it," Rudi said from one of the beds.

Tomás turned from the room's entertainment centre. "Is there always so much waiting involved?" he asked.

"Mostly." Rudi opened his eyes and looked at the cracked plaster of the ceiling for a few moments before sitting up. "What time is it?"

Tomás glanced at the clock in the bottom right-hand corner of the entertainment centre's screen. "Half past six."

Rudi sighed and regarded the little Portuguese sadly. "This is ridiculous," he said. "I've never had good luck in this city."

"You've been here before?"

"A few years ago." That time, he had been doing a favour for Wesoły Ptak, the organised crime gang to which the restaurant where he worked in Kraków paid protection money. This time at least he was involved in a proper Situation.

"How did that go?" asked Tomás.

Rudi considered the question. That Situation had eventually lasted a few days short of seventeen months and had involved half the mobsters in Europe pursuing him. He still had no clear idea how it had ended; people had simply stopped trying to abduct him and he had long since ceased to expect an apology for the mess. Normally, he wouldn't pass on operational information, but the whole business had left a sour taste that he was still trying to rid himself of.

"It was a fiasco," he said.

Tomás waited to see if more information was forthcoming. When none was, he got up from the threadbare sofa and padded barefoot over to the window. He was wearing cargo shorts and a thin white linen shirt, and a tiny gold cross on a thin chain tangled with the curly black hair on his chest. He lifted back the thin net curtain and looked down into the street. He didn't seem remotely nervous or apprehensive, which was good. Rather, he appeared mildly puzzled about what he was doing here. Which made two of them.

"Still there," he said.

Rudi got off the bed and went over to stand beside Tomás. The hotel was in a narrow little street some distance from the city centre; if one opened the window and stepped out onto the balcony and craned one's neck, one could just catch a glimpse, peeking over the roof of a credit union a few doors down, the cranes still surrounding one of the spires of the *Sagrada Familia*.

The street itself was choked with pedestrians and cars and those annoying little electric scooters which seemed unique to the city – Rudi had never seen them anywhere else, which he thought a blessing. On one of the buildings across from the hotel stood a huge billboard for a blockbuster film called *Texan Apocalypse*, which was a remake of an Estonian film called *Baltic Apocalypse!* which Rudi remembered from his childhood. The billboard featured burning vehicles and distant explosions and shadowy figures carrying ill-defined weapons. Below the billboard were several floors of balconies, each of them occupied by its own little garden of pot plants and herbs and trailing vines. And below those, at street level, was a brightly-striped canopy shading the tables of an outdoor café. At one of these tables, for some hours now, a man wearing chinos, a grey cotton jacket, and a Panama hat, had been sitting using a pad to read a newspaper.

Rudi had made him the moment he saw him, some vague sixth sense suggesting that here was someone to be noted, to be observed. "It's the hat," Tomás had said. "Who on Earth wears a Panama hat these days?"

For Rudi, it was more a matter of body language than anything else, but he had to agree that a Panama hat was something of an anachronism, and that made its wearer interesting. *I do not care if I stand out from the crowd*, the hat said. *I want you to know I am here.*

"Backup?" Tomás hazarded.

Rudi had shaken his head. There was no provision in his instructions for backup, although that didn't mean a great deal, particularly. If he'd learned anything over the past several years travelling hither and yon at the behest of Coureur Central, it was that everyone was continually winging it and half the time no one knew what anyone else was up to. It made, he supposed, for a suitably confusing environment for opposing forces, although it was hardly an optimal atmosphere in which to operate.

But he thought this was not the case here. The man in the Panama hat was not, he was certain, backup. He might, conceivably, be part of someone else's operation, nothing to do with them, but Rudi had long since given up believing in coincidence. Coincidence was for fools and optimists.

No, the man in the Panama hat – Rudi couldn't see his face from this angle but he thought he might be of a certain age – was there for them, and he was not backup. The easiest explanation was that he represented one part of the transaction for which they were waiting, ensuring that the Coureur was in place and ready to receive the Package. Which was unusual, in Rudi's experience, but not unheard-of.

"If he drinks any more coffee his heart's going to start dancing the Macarena," said Tomás.

"Hmm," said Rudi. Maybe the man in the Panama hat was waiting for him to go out and say hello? Maybe the Situation would not move forward until they had made contact? He had no code phrases or contact strings for such a contingency, but the temptation was growing stronger. "Ah, fuck this. Let's have something to eat."

Organising an Olympiad, in these Autumnal post-European days, was commonly regarded as something of a game of Russian Roulette. Quite apart from the cost, which could be ruinous, there was the ever-present question of whether a city, having been awarded the right to host the Games, would even be in the same nation four or eight years later to stage them.

This had led the International Olympic Committee to issue an edict that only nations which had been in existence for more than a decade – and there were those who felt that even this was perilously brief – would be allowed to bid for the Games. Catalunya, still opening its eyes and shaking itself a little at the suddenness of its independence, had just barely qualified, and Barcelona had put in a hosting bid more as a statement of nationhood than anything else.

Fortunately – or unfortunately, depending on how you looked at it – the only other bids that year had come from Dushanbe, Doha, and Pyongyang. The North Korean bid had been generally regarded as satirical in nature, although it was never easy to be sure when it came to North Korea. The other two bids – Doha was basically bankrupt and Dushanbe was... well – were never going to fly, despite slick presentations, and so Barcelona had found itself facing its second Olympics.

This had amused the international community in general and Spain in particular, which had been waiting for Catalunya to fail and come creeping back into the national fold. The cost of the Olympics had driven more than one city and several small countries to the wall. But Catalunya had been ticking along quite nicely; it hired a smart, aggressive organising committee, brought the Games in ahead of schedule and under budget, and branded them The Independence Games, which wiped the smile off the Cortes.

None of which was obvious to Rudi, walking down Carrer de Roger de Flor not far from Gaudi's cathedral. The streets were full of people dressed in various items of national costume, Olympic kit and football shirts, singing and waving flags and posing for selfies in the middle of the road, to the fury of local drivers. It was a dull and overcast day, with occasional spits of rain, but that didn't seem to be dampening anyone's spirits. Rudi supposed he ought to be charitable and feel pleased that they were having a good time.

He'd always liked the city, anyway. There was a peculiar density to it which he found somehow comforting, even if that density had been supersaturated by the invading army of sports fans of all nations.

The influx of people, and their megatonnes of hard currency, was also good news for the still-infant state. It was less good news for someone like Rudi, who had a list of restaurants he wanted to visit while he was here and was finding every single one packed to overflowing with diners of all nations.

They finally found a place on Carrer de Sicília, a bright, airy space with, for some reason which was not immediately apparent, several ancient and eye-hurtingly-polished Hispano Suizas parked among the tables. The maître d' led them to a table deep in the restaurant, in a corner which would have been secluded if the place hadn't been full of laughing, shouting, singing Olympic tourists wearing teeshirts emblazoned with the English flag.

"The Cross of St George," Tomás noted after they had been seated. "St George was either Greek or Roman, and he was born in Syria. I'll never understand the English."

"Hmm," Rudi said, deep in contemplation of the menu. He looked up. "I had a terrific meal the last time I was here, but I was barely in town long enough to enjoy it."

"What, here? In this restaurant?"

"No, somewhere else."

"Perhaps we should have gone there?"

"We couldn't afford it; we've barely got enough operational funds for this meal as it is. Whatever the hell is going on, it's not being run by people who like to spend their money."

This last was so pointedly directed at Tomás that he sat back in his chair. "I'm sorry," he said. "I have been presuming that you were properly briefed."

"That would be a first."

Tomás was a former priest, a Jesuit defrocked for some transgression which he acknowledged but was unwilling to specify. He was in his late thirties or early forties, a lithe and attentive man with a sense of amused stillness about him, as if he was patiently awaiting the punchline to a particularly involving joke. He had been introduced to Rudi yesterday as a Consultant, someone who would assess the validity of the Package before Rudi took delivery of it. This had never happened to Rudi before, and he was justifying it to himself as yet another strange little wrinkle of Coureur business.

Les Coureurs des Bois, for whom Rudi did occasional work when he wasn't cheffing in Kraków, carried items of mail across the continually reconfiguring borders of Europe's many new states and polities and countries and principalities. Sometimes, the items were illegal at their point of origin or their point of destination, or somewhere in-between, but mostly they were mundane and blameless. One thing they all had in common, however, was that the Coureur carrying them did not know what they were. Opening the Package either before or during transit was strictly anathema.

"I'm an expert in antiquities," Tomás said. "Specifically, religious relics. The people I represent want me to assess the bona fides of the item in question before it's transported."

"And that couldn't have been done before?"

"Apparently not. The vendors are being awkward; they refused to make the item available until the handover. A very large sum of money is involved."

"Of course there is." Rudi looked at the menu again. "And the item is a religious relic?"

"Well, that's for me to judge. The vendors claim it is."

Rudi glanced around the restaurant. A young woman in formal dress was sitting at a grand piano, playing something for the diners, but she was fighting a losing battle against the singing of the English tourists. "You seem as surprised to be doing this as I am."

Tomás shrugged. "I do this all the time, but it's usually for museums and churches and religious groups. Quite often for private collectors. This is a new situation for me."

"Every day," Rudi told him, "is a new Situation."

The meal, it turned out, was excellent. Rudi had the loin of lamb in a thyme crust, Tomás monkfish tempura. Dusk was beginning to fall on the city as they stepped out of the restaurant. The air was humid, and there was a light drizzle. A little further down the street, blue lights were strobing.

As they drew closer, they could see ambulances and police cars pulled up along the kerb. A motorcycle cop in ballistic armour and a heads-up helmet was taking statements from a group of people standing outside a café, and a little further down the street was taped off. Rudi could see one car apparently parked in a cavalier fashion, its bonnet crumpled against the front of an apartment building. A few metres away, a small white delivery van had come to a complete stop in the middle of the street, the lights and indicators of its rear nearside entirely sheared off in a bouquet of carbon composites.

Closer by, at the side of the road, was the detritus of paramedics, bloodied dressings, torn medical packaging, discarded surgical gloves.

Rudi stood and regarded the scene for some little while. Then he said, "We are going to walk. We are not going to run. We are going to catch the bus back to our hotel and we are going to check out. Then we are going to find somewhere else to stay."

Tomás looked surprised. "We are? Is something wrong?"

"I have no idea," said Rudi, "but I think it would be prudent." He nodded towards the gutter, where a white Panama hat lay torn and dirty.

Of course, finding somewhere else to stay in a city that was hosting the Olympic Games was not a straightforward matter; they'd been lucky to find rooms in the first place. They wound up in a large, anonymous motel right on the edge of town, almost in L'Hospitalet, where a convention of extremely grumpy businessmen appeared to be taking place. Their room was on the ground floor, tucked away down a corridor which ended in the loading bay for the kitchens. It had a single bed and a sofa and all the generic amenities familiar to the international business traveller. It was hardly luxurious, but Rudi did not plan on staying there for long.

While Tomás stood at the window gazing out at the disappointing view of the car park, Rudi made a crash call to an emergency contact number to apprise the vendors of the change of venue. The number cut straight to voicemail. He left a message.

An hour or so later, his phone received a text acknowledging his message and telling him that the vendors were on their way, and an hour after that there was a discreet knock on the door.

There were two of them, a man and a woman. Both middle-aged, both well-dressed. She was short and stout and annoyed-looking. He was tall and grey-haired and bearded and had the look of an academic. They didn't bother to introduce themselves, just completed the word-string recognition protocol. They both had Basque accents, and Rudi braced for trouble. This whole thing suddenly smelled of Politics; there had been a lot of upheaval in the Basque country lately.

"Why did you move?" asked the woman.

"I had a bad feeling," Rudi told her. "We were being watched. Was that you?"

The Basques shook their heads.

"Well," he said, "someone was keeping an eye on us, and they wound up as a casualty. You're lucky I didn't pull the whole thing and start again. Do you have the Package?"

The man was carrying a large plastic shopping bag printed with the name of a high-end fashion chain. Inside was a striped hatbox. He took it out and handed it to Rudi, who handed it in turn to Tomás, who was sitting on the sofa. Tomás's luggage consisted of an overnight bag and a fat attaché case. From the case, he took a large grey velvet cloth, which he spread on the room's coffee table. He also took from the case a pad and a pair of white cotton gloves, which he put on before lifting the lid of the hatbox and reaching inside.

The object in the box was wrapped in a layer of bubble-plastic, then a layer of wrapping paper, then several layers of cloth, which Tomás unwrapped carefully, setting each layer aside before starting on the next one.

This obviously annoyed the Basques. The woman said, "Will this take long?"

"It will take," Tomás said, "as long as it takes. You wouldn't want me to make a mistake, would you?"

The woman snorted.

Rudi had been expecting an ikon, or perhaps a statue, but what emerged as Tomás removed the final layer of cloth was a human skull, elaborately decorated with gold and what looked to be precious stones. There were two large faceted carnelians in its eye sockets and a line of pearls along the jaw. Tomás held the skull up and turned it this way and that, and then he put it down on the velvet cloth and sat looking at it. Someone had obviously taken a great deal of time and effort with the skull; it had once been gilded, but that had worn away in places. From where he stood beside the Basques, Rudi could see a large jagged hole in the skull's left temple.

Tomás took from his case a small battery-powered reading lamp. He placed it on the table and switched it on and looked at the skull some more. He took photographs with his phone. He seemed particularly interested in some marks on the back, and he took several photos of those.

"The skull of St Magnus Martyr, of Kirkwall," the Basque man said to break the silence.

Tomás picked the skull up again. "In 1578, vineyard workers in Italy discovered a catacomb containing a huge trove of skeletal remains," he said conversationally as he tipped it this way and that under the light. "There was, of course, no way back then to ascertain how old they were. It was assumed that they dated back to the early years of Christianity, and the obvious assumption was that at least some – perhaps all – of them had been martyred." He put the skull back down on the velvet cloth and sat looking at it, his hands in his lap. "This discovery was wonderful news for the Church. The rise of Protestantism had meant many Catholic churches were looted of their holy relics, and the Church has always found great strength in relics. And here was a new resource from which to restock them."

Rudi glanced at the two Basques, who had suddenly become quite impassive.

"So the catacomb was ransacked," Tomás went on. "A lot of the remains wound up in churches in Southern Germany, where nuns would adorn them with jewels, and they would be put on display, and the congregation could worship in the knowledge that they were in close proximity to a saint." He picked up the skull again and smiled apologetically across the room. "This is not the skull of Saint Magnus," he told them. "I would suggest that it came from the catacomb on the Via Salaria. It may belong to an early Christian martyr, it may not. But what I can tell you with some assurance is that it is the skull of a woman."

The Basques didn't move a muscle.

Tomás carefully rewrapped the skull, put it back into the hatbox, and replaced the lid. "My principals will not pay for this," he told them. "You have had a wasted journey."

The woman said, "How can you be certain this is the skull of a woman, just by looking at it for five minutes?"

Tomás sighed and took off his gloves. "In a previous life, the Church chose to send me to examine miracles," he said. "Back in the Sixteenth Century, one could say pretty much anything was a miracle and no one would disbelieve you, but these days the standard of proof is somewhat higher. Rome has to be careful. I've seen more of these –"

he tapped the box with a knuckle "– than I can quite remember, and I have learned to tell the skull of a woman from that of a man. It's actually quite straightforward. But I can run a genetic profile in a few minutes – I have the equipment with me – if you need scientific proof."

Some nonverbal communication seemed to pass between the Basques. The woman said, "We're not taking it back."

"Oh, now wait a minute," Rudi said. "This happened to me before and I spent almost a year and a half running around Europe with a piece of stolen merchandise. I'm not doing that again. Take this thing back where it came from and tell whoever gave it you that it's not what they think it is."

"No," said the man.

"Fine," said Rudi. "Fine. We can just leave it right here and let Housekeeping clear it up. I'm not taking it anywhere."

There was an awkward silence which lasted quite a long time.

Finally, the man said, "We are in a difficult position."

"Oh, for fuck's sake," Rudi said. "You stole it."

The Basques glanced at each other.

"No," said Rudi. "No, we are not getting involved in this. The skull isn't what you say it is and frankly you must be out of your minds to try a scam like this. What on Earth were you thinking?"

"Do you think," the man asked Tomás, "*anyone* would buy it?"

Tomás shrugged. "I couldn't begin to answer that. I can only speak for my principals, and they will not."

"It belongs to someone very powerful," the woman said.

"Then the best thing you can do is return it to them and hope they're in a forgiving mood," Rudi told them.

There was another long, awkward silence.

"No," Rudi said. "Absolutely not."

"Frankly, I'm amazed they thought they could get away with it," said Tomás.

"Some people are too stupid to be criminals," Rudi said. "Most people."

"This is the problem with the Church," Tomás said. "People – non-believers – think faith is the same as gullibility."

"I'd have thought that was axiomatic."

"You'd be surprised. Who are we waiting for?"

"I consulted with *my* principals," said Rudi. "They're sending a firefighter."

"Beg pardon?"

"I can't get involved in this thing," Rudi told him. "I was contracted to come here, have you assess the Package, and if it proved kosher, jump it to its final destination. What we're doing now is outside my remit; it needs another level of management."

Tomás raised an eyebrow. "Your boss is coming?"

"No. But someone with authority to resolve the situation is."

They were sitting on the grass in front of the Fundació Joan Miro, beside a rather jolly sculpture of red metal petals. Rudi had bought a bottle of Catalan pinot noir and some bread and cheese and they were watching the world go by.

"Do you think they'll be able to?" Tomás asked. "Resolve it?"

Rudi shrugged. "Not my problem."

"Is this your friend?" Tomás said, nodding at a tall young woman who was walking in their direction.

"I don't know. Let's see."

The young woman walked right up to where they were sitting and looked down at them, smiling sunnily. "Is that the local pinot?" she asked in English, pointing at the bottle of wine.

"Yes, it is," said Rudi, going along with the contact string.

She nodded. "Any good?"

"No, it's awful. Would you like a glass?"

The woman beamed. "I'd love one; I'm parched. Hi, I'm Victoria." She sat down opposite them and crossed her legs.

Rudi poured wine into a plastic cup and offered it to her. "Nice to meet you."

Victoria had long brown hair and hazel eyes. She tasted the wine. "Nice," she said. "I'll have to get myself a couple of bottles." She had a very, very faint West Country accent. "So, you have a problem."

"No," said Rudi "But someone we know does."

She shrugged. "Walk away from it. We're not a charity. Fuck 'em."

"May I say something?" asked Tomás.

"Absolutely," she told him. "We're all friends here."

Tomás took a moment to gather his thoughts. He said, "All this time, everyone has been treating the... Package as just a piece of merchandise, and I find that offensive. It may not be what my principals were told it was, but it was once a human being like you and me."

Victoria grunted. "Second Century Roman Christian martyr," she said. "Not *quite* like you and me."

"She may have been a martyr, she may not," he told her. "I seriously doubt whether we'll ever know. But she *was* a person, not a parcel to be passed from hand to hand like something in a children's party game."

Victoria nodded. "What's that cheese like?" she asked.

"Pretty good," said Rudi. "Help yourself." He handed the paper plate to her, and she cut herself a slice.

"Do you know those conversations that begin *I'm not a religious person?*" Tomás asked. "Well, I *am* a religious person. I believe in the sanctity of life and I believe everyone deserves dignity."

"Your principals obviously don't think that way," she pointed out, nibbling at the slice of cheese.

"It's not the first time we've had a difference of opinion," he said, and she chuckled. "My point," he went on, "is that in all probability, if we don't do something to take charge of this situation, the... *Package* is going to wind up thrown in a river or dumped in a garbage bin. I don't know who it originally belonged to, but if we can possibly return it, we should."

"Suppose it originally belonged to a sect of baby-eating Satanists?" she asked.

"Did it?"

"No, but suppose it did. Suppose it was being used in awful rites to bring about the ascendancy of the Devil on Earth – you do believe in the Devil, I suppose?"

"I believe in evil," Tomás said carefully.

"How about good? Do you believe in good?"

"Now that," he told her, "is a harder thing."

Victoria popped the last of the cheese into her mouth and chewed thoughtfully. "This *is* pretty good, you know. I like it here; everything I've eaten so far has been brilliant. The Poznań thing," she said to Rudi. "That was you, right?"

The Poznań thing had been a Situation which had gone so badly wrong that Rudi had wound up being tortured, until Central had intervened to extract him. He still had nightmares about it.

"We're sorry that happened," she said.

"So I was told," he said.

"You're not bad at what you do," she went on. "You've got pretty good judgement. What do *you* think we should do about this thing?"

"Me?" he said, surprised.

"Sure. Do we return the thing to the baby-eating Satanists and let them establish the dominion of their lord Lucifer? Or do we let the thieving scumbags run away and chuck it in a bin?"

"You'll excuse me if I tell you that this conversation is not going quite as I anticipated," Rudi said.

Victoria laughed and cut another chunk of cheese. "I presume the thieving scumbags still have the thing?"

"They were very keen to give it to us, but I didn't think that was a good idea," said Rudi.

"Dead right. You'd never have seen them again and it would be your problem. Which it is anyway." She looked at them. "We'll arrange for a dead-drop. The original owners can pick it up themselves. The thieving scumbags would be best advised to make themselves scarce and not trouble anyone else for the rest of their lives. How does that sound?"

"And you can facilitate this?" asked Tomás.

"Piece of piss," Victoria said cheerfully. "Nothing easier. You just have to know the right people to talk to, that's all."

Rudi suspected it wasn't quite that simple, but sometimes diplomacy had to be carried on at levels invisible to the footsoldiers. He said, "Someone died."

"Not died," Victoria told him. "He's in hospital. He'll be okay."

"What was that all about?"

"Ah," she said, reaching out for the bottle and pouring herself some more wine. "Now, that's the interesting thing about this business. On the face of it, you have a couple of thieving scumbags who stole something they couldn't sell and now they want to give it back in return for their miserable lives. But it turns out that someone else is interested in the Package too."

"Who?"

"Don't know. The chap who was keeping an eye on you is an independent contractor; he was hired by an anonymous party. Looks to us as if someone *else* tried to take him out, for reasons unknown."

Rudi stared at her.

"Anyway, don't tell the thieving scumbags. They have no idea just how fucking lucky they are to be getting out of this alive."

Tomás said, "We should, really..."

"As soon as they don't have the Package any more, they cease to be important," she told him. "Snatching someone and torturing them and killing them, that's a lot of effort. People would rather not do it if they don't have to."

"Well," Rudi demurred, "quite often an example has to be made. *Pour decourageur les autres.*"

Victoria waved it away. "We're not talking about some tuppeny-ha'penny street gang here," she said. "These people have class; they don't suffer from penis issues."

"And what about us?" Tomás asked. "Are we in any danger?"

Victoria guffawed. "Christ no, Father. You two just witnessed a car crash and went to help. Nobody's upset with *you.*"

Tomás thought about it. "May I ask," he said, "who the Package originally belonged to?"

Victoria grinned at him. "Well, you can *ask.*" And she laughed. When she realised no one else was laughing, she said, "No, I can't tell you. Best not to know."

This was good enough for Rudi, although the man in the Panama hat was going to niggle at him for a long time. "When shall we do it?"

"No time like the present," she said.

The Basques had obviously been arguing between themselves while they waited at the motel, but they were contrite, not wanting to meet anyone's eye, even when Victoria lectured them and called them 'muppets'.

"Idiot people," she told them. "Have you any idea how much trouble you've caused? And for what? You're no better off. Jesus fucking Christ on a fucking bike. Where is it?"

The Basque woman nodded at the coffee table, on which sat the box.

"Fine." Victoria went over and picked up the box. "Well, fortunately for you, *adults* are going to take over now and tidy up after you." She glared at the couple. "Now fuck off and don't fucking do it again." And she actually waited for the Basques to realise they'd been dismissed and shuffle out of the room.

In the silence that followed, Rudi and Tomás looked at

each other and wondered quite what they had witnessed. It was a little like, Rudi thought, seeing an angel of the Lord descending from Heaven with a flaming sword, but possibly he'd been spending too much time lately thinking about saints and faith.

When the Basques had gone, Victoria turned to them and smiled like the sun rising over a distant range of mountains. "Boys," she said, "go home. You did good. I'll take it from here."

Had they not actually had to go there, Rudi would have counselled avoiding the bus station entirely. It was a Babel of thousands of people, all trying to get to various Olympic events around the city and elsewhere in Catalunya, overwhelming the red-teeshirted stewards who were there to help everyone get where they wanted to go. The place looked like a riot. On the other hand, from an operational standpoint, it was a golden opportunity. Chaos was the great camouflager. He and Tomás were just two more bodies in a great sea of confused people. And even when they had made their way to the stands where the international coaches departed they were perfectly anonymous. In Coureur operational lore, busy bus stations were ideal arenas for all manner of transactions.

They walked for a while, looking for the gate from which Tomás' coach to Toulouse was due to leave, and when they found it they stood there, gazing around at the surrounding madness. Rudi strongly suspected that Toulouse was not Tomás' final destination, and he did the little man the professional courtesy of not asking.

"Well," Tomás said, "that was a peculiar couple of days."

"I've had worse," Rudi told him, and meant it.

"The Poznań thing?"

"That was different. But yes."

Tomás shook his head. "You're still young. Things will settle."

Rudi thought that, on previous experience, this was

unlikely. He said, "You would be doing me a considerable favour if you would explain some of what happened here."

Tomás laughed. "We're doomed to understand perhaps ten percent of what goes on around us; perhaps it's better that we get used to that as quickly as possible and not worry about the other ninety percent."

"Someone else said something like that to me once," said Rudi.

Tomás put his bags down beside his feet. "You understand that this business was about holy relics," he said.

"Yes."

"Relics are a tricky thing," Tomás said. "A damaged skull and some bones were found in a box hidden in a cavity in a column at St Magnus Cathedral in Kirkwall in 1919. According to the story of Magnus' death, he was executed by being struck on the head with an axe, and for the past century and a bit the bones found at the Cathedral have been believed to be his. It would annoy the people of Orkney quite a lot if a rival skull turned up all of a sudden in Barcelona, but I expect they would survive. The Scottish are no longer a particularly pious people. The publicity might even bring some more tourists into the area."

"So?" said Rudi.

"My principals, the people to whom I report, take this sort of thing *very* seriously. It's a matter of... of *heritage*, of the legitimacy of history. The bones at Kirkwall link the place back to the time when Magnus Erlendsson was Earl of Orkney. It's said he was so pious that he refused to fight. At one battle he stayed on board his ship and sang psalms."

"He sounds extremely annoying," Rudi mused.

"The point being," Tomás went on, "that if the relics at Kirkwall are not those of St Magnus, if they are not a physical link to him, then all the stories about him are simply myths. He might as well be Robin Hood or King Arthur."

This sounded uncomfortably like the kind of angels-dancing-on-the-head-of-a-pin discussion Rudi had spent most of his life trying to avoid, but he made the effort. "So whoever has the *real* skull has a certain amount of leverage."

"With my principals, yes. History is a strange thing; it keeps being written and rewritten and overwritten and rewritten again. They're looking for concrete evidence, historical markers. *This* man was *here*. He did *this*. *This* thing proves it. Do you understand?"

"It sounds as if your *principals* have chosen a thankless task for themselves."

"That's not for me to say. All I do is go where I'm sent and do as I'm told."

"And someone is trying to prevent them doing that?" Rudi asked, thinking about the man in the Panama hat. "Someone wants to stop them verifying history?"

"I imagine there are those for whom it would be better left unverified," Tomás mused. "For one reason or another. I don't know who they are."

"One would be inclined to suspect your former employers."

Tomás sniffed.

"This all sounds very Dan Brown, you know," said Rudi. "No offence."

"If it makes you feel better to think of it like that, go ahead."

"Is that why you left the Church? Because they didn't like you doing this?" He saw the look on the little man's face and instantly regretted opening his mouth. "Please," he said. "You don't have to answer that. Forgive me for asking."

Tomás shook his head, and for a moment Rudi thought he wasn't going to say anything at all. He picked up his bag and looked down the echoing length of the bus station. "For years I investigated charlatans and unmasked conmen," he said. "And that was good. It was important work. And one day I discovered a real miracle and the Church declared it a Heresy. So we had a problem, the Church and I."

"A real miracle?"

"Better you don't know," said Tomás. He smiled at Rudi. "Seriously, my friend. The world is not as you believe, and I pray you never discover just how much it is not as you believe." He put out his hand. "And now I must catch my bus. It has been a pleasure."

Rudi shook his hand. "Likewise. Will you be okay?"

"Me?" Tomás looked surprised. "Yes, of course. I did my job, everyone is happy. Why should I not be okay?"

Rudi had thought he'd seen a flash of anger in the little man's eyes when he talked about his Miracle, something fathomless and unresolved, the sort of anger which could easily break a person if they let it. "Just take care, Tomás, okay?"

"Sure." Tomás grinned at him. "You too." And he turned and walked away towards his bus.

A year or so later he was back in the kitchen at Restauracja Max. He'd more or less forgotten about the Situation in Barcelona; if he thought about it at all, it was as one more of the low-level snafus which seemed to characterise his Coureur life. Shortly after returning from Catalunya, he'd seen reports on the news of a series of truck bombings in the Basque country, and he'd wondered idly whether the skull had been offered for sale to raise money for those. Coureur Central tried its best to remain apolitical, but it was always hard to know exactly what cause the proceeds of a transaction were going to. He had carried out a search for the skull, but it seemed to have dropped entirely out of history, and as far as he was concerned it could stay that way.

One evening, the mafioso Dariusz turned up at the restaurant just after service, while the staff were cleaning up and Rudi was having a quiet post-mortem chat about the night's events with the kitchen crew. Dariusz was a representative of Wesoły Ptak, the man to whom Max, the restaurant's owner, paid his monthly protection money. He was also, by means never quite explained, Rudi's primary contact with Coureur Central.

"There's a job for you, if you want it," Dariusz told him

later over a glass of vodka, while Max's Filipina cleaning ladies hoovered. "Obviously you don't have to do it, but you were asked for by name. You must have impressed someone."

"May I ask whom?" Rudi said.

Darisuz chortled. "Well, you can *ask*," he said, and Rudi remembered someone else saying that, he couldn't remember quite who.

"Where is it?" he asked.

"Potsdam, in a week or so," Dariusz replied. "Better dress warmly; they're forecasting blizzards."

A Tale Of No City

Rodolfo Martínez

"What are you doing?"

As usual, Sarai appears out of nowhere and throws her question to the air as if she did not want an answer.

"A new building."

My words arouse her curiosity.

"What kind of building?"

"A church."

She frowns. Last week she heard about religion and insisted on learning everything about it, as she always does. She did not like it.

"We don't need a church."

"Don't use it as such," I say. "Use it as a playground or a museum, or... Well, as anything you like."

She does not seem convinced at all.

"Let me show you," I insist.

I display the blueprints and show her some old photographs I scanned a few days ago. Reluctantly, a spark of interest appears in her eyes. She tries hard not to be impressed, but she knows she isn't fooling me.

"All right," she concedes. "It seems nice. Where are you going to put it?"

I upload the city map and show her.

"There," I say. "At this spot, between Marina and Provença Streets."

"There's nothing there."

"But there was. And there will be."

She frowns again. Then, without a word, she disappears. I smile and go back to work.

Morning passes quickly. It is midday before I notice. I go to the refrigerator, take a can of food and a bottle of water and go to the roof. It is a pretty autumn day and no cloud stains a sky as blue as a dream. Behind me, what once was the National Park of Serra del Collserola is now an entangled jungle full of disturbing noises. In front of me the slope descends into the city in ruins until it dies in the sea. Sun reverberates in the quiet Mediterranean waters and everything around me seems to be asleep.

I open the can and eat without tasting the food. When I finish I drink the fresh water in the bottle at a gulp. I put can and bottle in a bag and, as every afternoon, I check the solar panels. All of them seem to be fine and I end my inspection with a shrug.

I go back into the building. I sit again and continue working until the dusk transforms everything around me into ghosts.

I get up, take a good look around and decide to go for Sarai as I do every night.

The city is a delicate gem, a flower always on the brink of blooming. In the beginning, long before I let my siblings get out and wander its streets, it was just an empty landscape, contoured by the sea to one side and the distant mountains to the other. I know the original has no such mountains, but I added them because they provide a good point of reference and come in handy to delineate the borders.

I began to construct the first buildings five years ago and two years later I released my siblings into the streets. There are still too many empty spaces but I do my best to keep them out of sight. I usually succeed and my siblings are not aware of all that is missing in the landscape. For them, the city is complete, and it has always been that way.

Not for all of them, of course.

Sarai is different. She is fully aware of the empty spaces. And she recognizes the new buildings as such when I add them. As witness her words this morning. Nobody has ever noticed that there is nothing between Marina and Provença Streets, that the place where once the Sagrada Familia stood is just an empty spot full of darkness and noise.

Not for long, I tell myself.

"You're late," says Sarai, appearing suddenly by my side.

"You're early," I reply.

She smiles, though my words are exactly the same as last night's and the night before's. As usual, she looks like a teenage girl with tousled ginger hair and mischievous green eyes. She is tall, a little taller than me, and looks skinny at first sight, but that impression vanishes quickly. She has strong cheekbones and a stubborn jaw that always trembles when she is about to acknowledge she is wrong.

We walk by the darkened streets without saying a word. This part of the city is almost empty and the moon seems to be playing hide-and-seek with the tall buildings. We descend to Via Augusta and turn right to Montaner Street until we arrive to Diagonal Avenue. We see groups of people here and there. Some of them are sitting in a circle, discussing passionately something we cannot hear, and some are walking lazily and pausing every few steps. I see Provença Street to my left, but I pretend to go straight as if ignorant of where Sarai is taking us. Impatient, she takes my arm and leads me to Provença. I smile and notice she is making a great effort not to do the same.

We arrive at last. There are not many people around us those that are cannot see the empty space we are looking at. A cluster of clouds hides the moon and suddenly the entire world transforms into a cold empty space. The moment passes as quickly as it came and I wonder if I imagined it. A glitch in the system, maybe. I will have to check later.

"Did you know the original Sagrada Familia was never finished?" asked Sarai, who does not seem to have noticed anything untoward.

I nod. She has been reading the database. Not that I would have expected otherwise.

"And did you know that it was financed by private investment?"

I nod again. Sarai's questions are not a surprise. I was

expecting something of the sort since this morning. I am sure she has been researching most of the day, with every piece of discovered information increasing her curiosity.

"But I don't want it to be a church," she says. Her voice is now firm, sharp, and she is ready for a long battle.

"Then it won't be a church."

She stumbles, as if she had pushed too hard against a wall that wasn't there.

"All right," she says, frowning. I guess she is waiting for the catch. There is no catch, but she doesn't know that.

"Great," I say. "Can we go on with our walk?"

Not entirely convinced she has won before the battle even started, she nods. I savor the moment; surprising Sarai is not something that happens every day. She takes a couple of steps, stops suddenly and turns to me.

"It was as if the building belonged to everybody," she says. "To all that had participated in its financing, at least. Wouldn't be great if we could do something like that with this one?"

"Of course," I say. "We can make a public call and people can donate…"

"No, not *just* this. Not money. Something more personal."

"Like what?"

"Their work. Let them erect the building, dig the foundations, raise the walls, decorate the… Let them make it with their own hands."

Now it is my turn to be taken by surprise. Where does she get these crazy ideas from? I consider it for a moment. I like it, but…

Sarai is staring at me. She looks nervous, almost anxious, as if her future depended on my response.

I consider her proposal at length. The idea is appealing, but at the same time it implies changing everything around us. Until now, my siblings have been living a perpetual *now*, without memories of the past or desires for a future. What Sarai is proposing would change everything. She is talking about a process that will last months, maybe years. The citizens will see the Sagrada Familia growing up before their eyes and they will have a landmark to show the passage of time. They will be conscious of the past. They will imagine the future. They will change, they grow older, they...

Nothing will be the same.

But, is this not exactly what the Parents intended when they put me in charge? Sooner or later, my siblings will have to leave their perpetual present and begin to live a real life.

Has the moment arrived?

The answer is waiting for me in Serai's eager green eyes.

I knew this moment would come, but I expected it to arrive later. When I'm older, maybe wiser.

But what Sarai proposed makes sense. It is the next logical step. The only step I can take, in fact. I have known it for some time, but I have been postponing it again and again.

It was one of the very first things the Parents told me when they began to train me.

"For them to have a real life, they must have a past and a future. They must grow up, get older. And they must die."

I remember vividly their long solemn faces, the five of them.

"Someday they will be ready. You must decide when."

Is now the time? One part of me wants to insist not: they are not ready, it is too soon. But even that part of me knows deep down that I am lying and they have been ready for some time now.

From the roof, I gaze at the lazy clouds. Below me brushes, weeds and trees are the new masters of what once was a city, a jungle that spreads its arms around the frame of a dead body. I finish my lunch and make a decision.

Good-bye, Sarai, I think as I walk down. Good-bye my stubborn child, my sweet, innocent, wicked girl. In the blink of an eye you will be a full grown woman, and your head will be filled with hundreds of things more interesting than spending time with me.

The rest of the day passes with me revising calculations and implementing new algorithms. I check them rigorously and when I am sure everything is right I stop the running of the city and wait while the system saves a backup of its actual status.

All lights are green. Everything is ready. I upload the new algorithms and integrate them into the system. I wait a few eternal seconds with my finger hanging over the EXECUTE key and I finally strike it with a desperate rage that vanishes in quiet resignation.

The city is running again. Its citizens are waking up without knowing they have been asleep. Their clock starts ticking. They begin to live.

The first time I plugged myself to the digital world and played with my digital siblings I was only a child. It was amazing. I was not alone; there were other children like me and I could play with them. Everything seemed more real than the flesh and bone world, more vivid, more intense. My siblings were little more than babies and they were full of curiosity and eager to know new things. My arrival was like a birthday present for them. Of course they had met the Parents, but the gap between them was too big. I could interact with them far more effectively than an adult.

Once I returned to the flesh and bone world I asked Aurora why I could not remain there forever. She shook her head and said, "You could. But then you couldn't help us develop your siblings."

I must confess the subject did not seem very important to me then. I was nothing more than an ignorant child, without a real sense of what was important and what was not.

"Besides, if you are going to be a permanent resident of the digital world you cannot remember who you are."

I did not understand.

"The system has safeguards to prevent certain things.

Among them, it prevents a person of this world taking his preconceptions with him. If you are going to be a permanent resident, the memory of your digital self will be erased, only your personality patterns would remain."

"I don't want to forget what I know."

"You would also forget who you are."

The public call to build the Sagrada Familia has been a tremendous success. There are just four hundred citizens and sometimes I have the feeling that every single one of them is at the site digging and working on the foundations.

Sarai is among them, of course. She stills walks with me at evenings and nights, but we walk now by streets full of people, anxious to celebrate their lives. And the construction of the new building is her main topic of conversation.

I did not expect anything else, but it hurts just the same.

I realise Sarai notices and tries to restrain her enthusiasm, but with limited success. She is happy, excited as I have never seen her. And why not? For the first time in her life she is truly alive.

Weeks pass and our relationship returns to normal… almost. Something is lost, but what it remains is enough, at least for now.

The foundations are advancing at a good pace and having something to construct together has given the citizens a sense of community they did not have before. I should be satisfied, exultant. The project has entered a new phase and I sense that in no time the citizens will be ready to fly by themselves.

But I am far from content. I do not mind they no longer need me, but I cannot bear the idea that someday Sarai will be able to manage all by herself and I will become just an appendix; nice but not essential and maybe even annoying sometimes.

Some nights I have the feeling she is reading my thoughts. There are moments she seems about to say something. But she always changes her mind and the words that hover on her lips vanish in the thin cool night air without a trace.

These are busy days, not only for the citizens but for me. I spend my mornings in the flesh and bone world fighting again unexpected bifurcations in the code and tracing all the programing modules, searching for bugs. Everything seems to be fine but, as one of the Parents used to say (was it Carles or maybe Roberto? I cannot remember), "Everything seems to be fine even a nanosecond before the collapse."

So I do not relax but work hard, harder than I have worked before. There are hundreds of thousands of code lines, some of them in almost unintelligible obsolete computer languages, and the integration of the entire system seems sometimes a Christmas tree designed by a drunk engineer.

After all, many of the pieces that are now part of the system were originally designed for other tasks. It is a miracle the Parents were able to assemble all this and make it work. I am a midget walking on the shoulder of giants, I am very conscious of that.

Another week passes by and I relax and try to enjoy this new phase of the project. Things seem to be fine. The foundations will soon be finished and Sarai and I are satisfied with the way things are developing... though that satisfaction is not entirely genuine. At least as far as I am concerned.

But we have found common ground when we walk and talk and look at each other. We can fool ourselves into thinking there is no one else around and nothing has changed. An illusion, we both know, but it's enough for the time being.

I remember last time Aurora and I talked. She was in her bed, which was about to become her shroud. Her head and one of her arms were plugged into the autodoc, whose lights were blinking frantically, passing quickly from green to red. She was the last of the Parents alive and she was infinitely old, the oldest person in the world she seemed to me. And maybe she was, who knows? The autodoc had been trying to keep her alive for the past week, but there was nothing more it could do.

She looked at me.

"You're on your own now."

I nodded. I could not talk. What could I have told her? Words were meaningless.

"I must go, my beautiful boy. It's time to rest."

I noticed the tears in my eyes but did nothing to wipe them away.

"Good-bye, my sweet prince," she said. Her green eyes looked at me one last time. She smiled. "Until our next meeting."

Those were her last words. One moment her eyes looked at me with something I like to think of as 'love', the next they were just two empty glass marbles.

From that moment on I was alone in the flesh and blood world. Forever, or so I thought.

"Hi! 'Body home?"

It is a young voice, one that sounds almost amused. For an instant I am convinced I have imagined it, until a silhouette appears in the threshold, framed by the outer light. I blink and shake my head.

I am awake and I am not hallucinating. It is another human being. A flesh and blood human being.

No, that is not possible. What are the odds? The war and the post-war fertility disease finished everyone... That was what the Parents used to tell me again and again, though Aurora admitted one day this was an assumption. They thought mass extinction was the most probable consequence, but had no way of being certain.

I stand up.

"Hi," I manage to say. "Welcome, *benvingut*."

My voice sounds harsh. It has been a while since I used it in the physical world. It seems an old man's voice. A drunk old man's voice, I tell to myself while I hold back a giggle.

"Wow! Ar'u real?"

I increase the light intensity and let him examine me thoroughly.

"Come in," I say. "You are welcome."

He still hesitates. Suddenly he bows and says,

"May'ur days'll be fill'd with joy and 'ur nights with excitement."

He seems to expect some kind of answer from me.

"Thank you," I say. "I desire the same for you. I don't know the proper words. I'm sorry."

He smiles while he slips inside and takes an amazed look around. Now that he is no longer backlit I can see that he is indeed a young man. Almost ten years younger than me, I would say. He seems to be about seventeen at most. He has nice and frank features, and is almost barefaced. A short blonde fuzz crosses his jaw and upper lip and his hair spreads upon his shoulders like a golden cascade.

"Fabri," he says pointing to his chest.

"Abraham," I reply, guessing he is telling me his name.

"Come from Novuporti. 'S south two days walk from here."

"I... I don't come from anywhere. I'm home," I say, and I notice my words surprise him.

"U... U'r born here, in *Barslona*?"

I do not correct his pronunciation. Why should I?

"Yes."

"U... no, 's impossible. U'r not old enough. U can't've known ancient world."

I smile and shake my head.

"I didn't. My Parents did, though."

He seems fascinated, not only by my words but by everything that surrounds him. He is like a child in a candy store. Well, he is in fact a child, no older than Sarai.

"Adulthood voyage's been more interesting than anticipated," he says, enthusiastic. "My folks won't believe when tell'em."

"Didn't you expect to find anyone here?"

"Of course didn't! This Barslona, ruins of ancient world. Nothing should live here. Should be no more than ghosts and specters…" Suddenly he bites his thumb and spits on his palm. "U'r no ghost… ar'u?"

I laugh.

"I'm a man, just like you," I say.

He walks towards me, not entirely convinced. He stretches one arm and touches my face. I let him do it and try to be as still as possible. He ends his inspection and nods, satisfied at last.

"Ye', u'r man. Ghosts don't sweat or breathe. Guess."

I smile, trying to be as soothing as I can. He smiles back. Suddenly I see a weird glow in his eyes.

"Do'u wanna've sex?" he asks, stammering.

"Just like that? Is that a custom among you when you meet a stranger?"

"Sometimes. When wanna be sure 's no ghost."

"I see. Why not? Follow me."

"This compound was created as part of the war efforts," Aurora told me once. We were alone. I suspect she would not have told me anything if the other Parents had been there. They did not like to talk about old times but there was nothing Aurora did not want to talk about. "We created drones and robots faster and more versatile than those existing ones. We learnt to play DNA as a virtuoso musician plays her instrument. We developed AI algorithms more complex than anyone could have imagined."

She stopped and looked me right in the eye, as if she wanted to be sure I understood everything she was telling me. I sat straight and did not blink.

"And that's why we couldn't leave. When everyone ran, when the world fell apart and there was nothing to live for, we didn't give up. We couldn't. What we had achieved…"

She pointed to the line of servers, to their blinking lights.

Her green eyes welled.

"They're alive. They think. They're people. Not just information, not just a bunch of ones and zeroes in a flow of data. Nobody intended to create them, but they exist. They are our children. No, not mine or the other Parents'. They are the children of humankind. They will inherit the world and, hopefully, they won't make the same mistakes we did."

I do not know how old she was. All five of them seemed terribly old to me when I was a child. But she had to be very old. Ninety? A hundred? Maybe more. She and the others had been working by their own so many years, trying to develop those digital children they had accidentally created. And in their last years they created a flesh and blood one. Me.

So old. Will I someday be as old as she was? Will I endure long enough?

He is sleeping now. I watch him and wonder what is he dreaming of. He is so young, just a boy, and in same strange way he reminds me of Sarai.

He turns round and faces me. There is a smile in his lips and his breathing is calm, regular. What kind of person is capable of sleeping like that in the presence of a stranger? What kind of community breeds people like that, so confident, so trustful?

After the sex we have been talking. He was curious about me and the place, of course. He said he was not expecting to find anyone in the old city. Only ruins and maybe ghosts. I told him a few things, nothing really important, and while I was talking I saw he could not stop looking at the blinking lights of the servers. *What are they?* he asked. *Machines,* I answered. *What kind of machines?* he wanted to know. *Machines that handle information,* I said.

His curiosity seemed boundless. But he was polite enough to curb it when I asked about him and his people.

They number just over a hundred and fifty, though a

traveller who came from the south five years ago told them there was a community of about five hundred people at the banks of Guadalquivir. That visit was the most thrilling moment Fabri and his people can remember. They are an agricultural community and have lost most of the technological knowledge of the ancient world. Fabri recalls they had electric light when he was a child, but not any more.

I did not dare ask if there are many youngsters like him among his people or if he was an exception. He would have found the question too weird and I did not want him to suspect anything strange. I told myself that a community so small was not genetically viable and tried to convince myself that, even if they could conceive and deliver as before the war, I should not be worried.

But I am. Of course I am.

I watch him again and consider the idea of trying to convince him to stay here and help me with the project. I could teach him and it would be gratifying to have a companion after all those years, someone who shared my goals, someone to talk to, to touch, to caress…

But I do not dare try. I cannot afford to take the risk.

He is innocent. He does not mean any harm. He is just an ignorant and enthusiastic child, eager to learn and to discover new places, not very different from my siblings. And when he returns to his community he will tell the others what he has found in the ancient city of Barslona and…

I cannot allow it.

The Parents were very specific regarding that. The viability of the project stands on secrecy. Humans must not know they are a dying species, much less that they have a replacement.

"If someone has survived they mustn't know what's happening here," Aurora told me time and again. "Not for the next thousand years at least, assuming they survive."

I can see her before me as if she really were here. Her

skin is like an old map road and her hands tremble, but her green eyes still keep the fire of youth.

She was right. No one must know.

And I know what I have to do.

Slowly, quietly, I put my knees on his shoulders, I bend down and pass my hands around his neck. Little by little, I begin to tighten. I try not to look at him but I cannot help it and my eyes stay fixed on his face.

He wakes suddenly and looks at me, incapable of understanding what is happening. He struggles, but I am strong. He opens his mouth, I am not sure if he is trying to breathe or if he wants to say something. It does not matter. The air will never reach his lungs and I do not want to hear anything he may wish to say.

There is a crunch. His eyes turn to cold glass. All struggle ceases. I relax, loosening my grip. His mouth is half open and there is a look of astonishment in his dead eyes. He has died without understanding why and he will never have the chance to do so. If there is an afterlife, as Carles thought (an idea Aurora heatedly refuted), he will spend it haunted by the knowledge that he will never understand why he died.

I wish I could have explained it to him, I wish...

I stand up and wipe the tears from my eyes. It is late in the night and I should sleep, but I must dispose of the body. It will be a hard and nasty work and the sooner I get to it the better.

Next day I walk around the compound and make a thorough inspection. The compound should have been effectively hidden, but Fabri had managed to find it. Even if it was only by chance I cannot take the risk of anyone else stumbling upon it. So I look for weak spots and try to find a way to strengthen them.

If someone walks by again someday he should not see anything of interest, just weed and brushes and the ruins of an old building. He should go on his way without taking a second look. I cannot afford another Fabri...

Why did he have to tell me his name?

I push aside the thought as firmly as I can. I have no time for this. I am going to be busy for the next few years, working not only on the developing of the digital world but on its protection from the physical world. Between them these tasks will consume all my waking time. I will have no time for anything else.

Why did he have to tell me his name?

"I've missed you"

I am about to say sorry, but I know that is useless with Sarai.

"I had things to do."

"Very important things, it seems."

"They were."

She hesitates for a moment and then she shrugs.

"What do you think?" she asks, pointing at the people working on the building. Foundations are finished and the walls are beginning to take shape. It is remarkable what they have achieved in the months I have not been here.

"It seems fine," I say.

"Better than fine. It has given us a common purpose."

I nod. "I know."

Yes, how could it be otherwise, I suspect she is thinking. As far as she is concerned I know everything. Sometimes I wonder if that is the only reason she began to talk to me, because I seemed to know everything.

When I began to plug myself into the digital world after the death of the Parents, I did so only because I wanted to see for myself how things were going... Or at least that was what I told myself. I tried to keep my interactions with the citizens at a minimum. And I managed to do so until she appeared.

"You're new," she told me the moment she saw me.

That aroused my interest. How could she know that? It should not have been possible for her to remember previous iterations of her world.

It did not take me long to discover that Sarai was unique in many ways. At first she only asked me questions, one after another. Surprised by the fact that I seemed to have an answer for everything, she redoubled her efforts and her questions became more complex and elaborate.

One day she asked me where I went when I was not there. That shocked me in ways I cannot describe. She should not have been aware of my absences.

I know I should have checked her records, examined her behaviour parameters and tested her access levels. I did not, afraid of what I might find.

By then, Sarai was the most important part of my world. I just could not risk discovering that her behaviour and her personality were the consequences of a system bug. Though there were far worse alternatives...

"What was the ancient world like?" I asked Aurora one day.

She smiled, a sad and homesick smile, and then stared at me with those green eyes. They were the eyes of a young woman, maybe a child. The only aspect of her that did not age.

"It was the best of times, it was the worst of times,", she said, as if she was reciting a verse. "It was the age of wisdom, it was the age of foolishness, it was the epoch of belief, it was the epoch of incredulity, it was the season of Light, it was the season of Darkness, it was the spring of hope, it was the winter of despair."

"I don't understand," I said, perplexed.

She shrugged and then did something no one had ever done to me before. She bowed and gave me a kiss.

"It was a time like any other," she said. "Just like any other."

The construction of the Sagrada Familia is progressing well. Very well, in fact. The original building took more than a hundred years and it was never finished. This one could be completed in a few months, a year and a half at most.

Everyone is working on the project and, in doing so, they are discovering new abilities. As work progresses they are beginning to differentiate one from another. Some of them discover they are good at maths, others develop unsuspected manual skills, still others... They are becoming more and more individual, each with a distinct personality and different abilities. And at the same time their bonds as a community are strengthened by the task.

Sarai was right. That kind of involvement was just what they needed to take the next step in their development. How could she know? And how could I not?

She looks at me and smiles, as if she is reading my mind. Sometimes I think she is. And, well, it is not impossible. Just now my thoughts are nothing more than data bits in the server cloud. Anyone can read them if she or he has the right access level. Has Sarai?

"You're paranoid," she tells me. Is she just joking or it is her way of telling me I am right?

"That doesn't mean nobody is after me," I answer.

She laughs. And her laugh is so genuine, so naïve that it puts an end to my suspicions... almost.

There is so much work to do.

The Parents were old people when I was born. And I was the only success in a long list of failed attempts. They had been working all their lives, trying to preserve the precious discovery they had made at the end of the war, just a few months before the fertility disease spread around the world.

"Humankind is doomed," they told me the minute I was able to understand them. "But there is another possibility, another form of life, another..."

Roberto, impatient as usual, pushed Carles aside and said:

"They are our children. Your siblings, in some ways. You must protect them and help them to develop."

There was so much I did not understand. But Aurora, more patient than the others, explained things to me until I understood.

She was my favourite Parent. Carles, Roberto, Farya and Chihook were fine, but Aurora... She never got impatient with me, she never thought I was not up to the task, she never refused to answer a question. She always paid attention to what I said and I could tell she was not merely being polite, she was really interested in what I had to say.

"We were lucky," she once told me. "This facility was secretly built in the last years of the war. Only a few knew of its existence and location, and it was designed to be self-sufficient. Sheer luck. Our discovery could have taken place in a less protected site... or nowhere."

She taught me to work hard, to never give up. But there is so much to do. And there are dangers I have not considered, as Fabri's visit has shown me.

I wish Aurora were here now. I could ask her. Because Sarai is wrong. I do not know everything; I do not have all the answers. Aurora and the others did. They were the creators of this world, I am just a gardener, a caretaker. Aurora would have known what to do.

But you do *know what to do*, her voice says inside my head. *You must protect your digital siblings. They are the future.*

What I do not know is if I will have enough time to do everything I must. And not only time. After all, I am only one person and there are so many tasks involved.

I can control the digital world, its programming and its developing. But what about the other machinery, the solar panels, the construction robots, the... So long as nothing serious happens I can take care of maintenance, and the machines were designed to repair themselves as well as other machines, but there are some things they cannot do, things that require a human hand. I am not sure mine are capable enough.

No matter how many years I live, sooner or later I will die. By then, my siblings have to be able to control not only their digital world but the machines of the physical world also. If a solar panel fails, they have to be capable of sending and controlling a drone to make reparations.

Yes, I worry too much. Before the arrival of Fabri I rarely thought about the future. As my siblings, I lived in a perpetual now and that was enough for me.

Things have changed. He has changed everything. Am I doing what I must? Is the world out there really a dying place without hope? Are Fabri's and the other communities that exist doomed to a long decay that can only end in extinction?

I have no answers. I have only memories of an innocent laughter and a pair of trustful eyes, of someone I killed before I really knew him.

But I cannot afford to hesitate now. Right or wrong this is my life, the one I know. I am the caretaker of the future, I tell myself, I must not give up.

But what future? I wonder. Not my future, but theirs. Fabri was lucky, I killed him in the prime of his life, he will not have to endure the indignities of old age. He will never grow old, his body will not betray him, he will not...

Enough. Enough. This is my life. Nothing else matters.

Time goes by. Weeks turn into months and months into years. The drones under my command have almost completed their tasks. When they finish it will be all but impossible for anyone to find this place... At least that is my intention. I have done my best. I hope it will be enough.

In the digital world the city develops fast and my digital siblings with it. They have taken matters into their own hands and now decide by themselves what to construct and where. The city is taking shape; the empty places are empty no more and new buildings are being erected.

The new city is very much like the original but it is not an exact copy. There are new places and streets and buildings, and even those that are like the old ones are slightly different. My siblings go on evolving and they are beginning to get creative. The Ramblas are a good example: they have transformed them into a series of pools, each them home to a different kind of fish.

The population grows as they learn to interact and create new life.

The Parents would be proud, I hope.

Though everything seems to be fine there is something that disturbs me. Something that it is not as it should be. And even though I rather like the anomaly it worries me in ways I cannot describe.

The compound is hidden and safe. The digital world has grown complex enough to almost develop by itself. My siblings grow up steadily.

All of them but one.

"You're not getting older."

"You are."

Sarai is right. My digital self reflects with painful fidelity the ten years that have passed. But she is the same teenage girl I met so many years ago. She has not changed a bit.

"This is how things are," I say. "All living things grow up, get older and, some day, die."

"Am I not alive, then?"

A good question. Is she alive? What is she?

"Not entirely," I answer, measuring every word. "Life is change. You must change if you want to be entirely alive."

She hesitates a moment. She shrugs.

"I'll change," she says.

"But not today."

"No, not today."

Her words fill me with joy… but they also scare me.

When I get back to the physical world I do what I have been avoiding all these years. I enter the system and look for Sarai parameters.

I fail.

Time and again the system stops me and tells me with its

annoyingly polite voice that I do not have the required security level.

I try to keep calm and not to wonder how it is possible for the only system administrator to not have a high enough security level. I will consider that question later, once I have solved the mystery of Sarai.

But despite every effort I fail. For two day I try and my frustration grows and grows after each failure.

I decide to go back to basics, to the beginning, to the original system specifications as the Parents wrote them.

I find what I am looking for after several hours of reading machine code. The system itself has the highest security level and can override any request by the administrator if it considers that request endangers the project. A programmer remark informs me that it was Aurora who implemented that code.

It makes sense. Not that I am capable of seeing that at first. But after a few hours working in the solar panel maintenance I can get back to the server room and face the problem with a cool head. Yes, it makes sense; the system has to be capable of defending itself against anything that threatens the parameters of the project. It does not matter if the thread is internal or external. In fact, internal threats may be even more dangerous than the external ones.

But that leaves an unanswered question. Why would my trying to see Sarai's parameters put the project at risk?

I spend the next two days designing a spy module. When it is ready for release I hesitate. Should I do it? What if the system is right and I am putting at risk everything the Parents and I have done? Is it so important for me to know what Sarai is that I am willing to endanger my life's work to find out?

Seconds turn into minutes and minutes are about to turn into an hour when I finally give the order.

Ten endless minutes later my spy module returns with the information it has managed to get.

Almost nothing. The system is shielded well enough to

protect itself from my feeble attempts to trespass. The only thing the module can give me is the creation date of Sarai's parameters and when she was activated.

Nothing. A trifle. What good is knowing the exact moment the Parents created and activated her?

But it is the only thing I have, so I open the file.

It cannot be. It makes no sense.

Sarai was created and defined several years after my other siblings. Many years later, in fact. Why? What happened? Did the Parents develop some new algorithm and implement it in Sarai? If so, why did they not tell me? I was alive and working when Sarai was defined and activated.

I was...

I make a quick mental calculation. The year, the month, the day. Yes, of course I was alive, but none of the Parents were... except Aurora. But not for long. She must have died a few days after...

Or was it the same day?

I upload Aurora's vital data. I look for the date and time of her death. When I find them I do not need to compare them with the date and time my module has retrieved.

Sarai was born less than a picosecond after Aurora's death.

The system has safeguards to prevent certain things, I recall. *Among them, it prevents a person of this world taking his preconceptions with him. If you are going to be a permanent resident, the memory of your digital self will be erased, only your personality patterns would remain.*

But that is not the only thing that remains, I tell myself. Maybe Sarai does not have my mother's memories, but she does have her access level to the system. That is why she was aware of time passing, and knew that I did not belong to the system. She is a preferential user, so she can do things my other siblings cannot.

Such as refusing to grow up and being a teenager as long as she wants, for instance.

An accident or did it happen deliberately? Had Aurora

tricked the system in some way to allow her digital self to become a super user?

A new memory comes out of the blue and strikes me suddenly. I see Aurora again, at the time of her death. I remember her last words to me:

"Until our next meeting."

She told me. She told me what was about to happen with her last words. I have been so stupid. A perfect and complete moron. All these years I had the truth in front of me and I did not see it.

Maybe I did not want to.

Time goes by. It is hard for me to distinguish one year from another. When I look back it seems only yesterday when the Parents died, when Fabri arrived, when my siblings began to build the city by themselves. A sigh. A blink.

But it has been twenty years since the Sagrada Familia was finished, since the first fireworks were launched to celebrate the completion of the building, since…

I am not a young man anymore and I have not been for several years. I am not as old as the Parents, but old enough to be younger than my body. My eyes reflect the passage of time, also. It has been a while since they seemed innocent and eager. And maybe those eyes I remember were not even mine, but Fabri's…

I am in good health. If I am careful, I have several years before me. *What kind of years?* I wonder. Living in a dead world and taking care of a newborn is not for me. My siblings will go on evolving, developing, building and changing their environment, creating their own universe as they explore it and imagine it. I… I will simply grow old and one day I will die. I will be as dead as the rest of the world.

As dead as Fabri.

Funny. As years go by I think more and more of Fabri and I wonder how things might have turned out had I made a different choice. Would I have been able to convince him to help me? Had I given him the opportunity, would he have seized it?

It does not matter. Not really. Thoughts and remorse cannot change the past. But these thoughts persist. Old man stuff, I guess.

In those twenty years my visits to the digital world have become less and less frequent. My siblings evolved quickly and in no time they were managing the world by themselves. A world whose shape has begun to change in ways I could not have imagined. After twenty years, the city has become something very different from the original.

Well, the original was a ghost invaded by the jungle when Fabri arrived and today it is nothing but than a distant memory.

Some things remain: the Sagrada Familia and a couple of other places that still hold meaning for the citizens. They are building their own city... If what they are building is in fact a city. Sometimes I have my doubts.

And why not? The Parents wanted them to be free of the mistakes of the ancient world. Yes, let them make their own mistakes. They are entitled to, after all.

During these years, Sarai and I have seen each other from time to time. She still looks like a teenager and behaves as one, but her eyes belong to an older person. Funny, because it was just the other way around with Aurora.

My work here is done and my presence is now more and obstacle than a help. Time to go; time for them to live their lives without outside interference, not even mine.

It is time for Sarai and I to say good-bye.

"You are leaving," she says the moment she sees me.

"I am. And it's time for you grow up. Thank you for having been the same for me all those years. There is no need for that anymore."

She does something I do not remember seeing her do before: she begins to weep. Quietly, solemnly, tears slip through her check.

"Shhh. It's all right," I say. "You need to live your lives

on your own. No more supervision. I will protect you until my last day, but I don't belong here. Not anymore. This is your world now."

She is about to say something. I am almost sure she is about to say this can be my world too, but she suddenly keeps quiet. All my plans fall down like a house of cards and I cannot say a word. So I keep watching her.

And do as you did, mother? I would have replied to the proposition she has not made.

I know she would not have been surprised by my words. I am positive that, in some way or another, she has learnt about herself... Well, I am not sure that 'herself' is the right word. The person whose thought and behaviour patterns were used to create her, then.

Maybe she would ask me how long I've known. What could I tell her? That I knew for a long time? That, in some ways, I always have known but I did not want to find out? All the clues were right there in front of me.

But it does not matter. Maybe she has inherited the personality patterns of Aurora, but she is not her. She is Sarai. And I have loved them both.

I take a long look around. One last look, at least with these weary old eyes. There are so many new things, so many changes, so many people. I guess I did my work well, after all, though sometimes I regret that the new city is not more like the original.

But why should it be? This is their world, not a ghost copy of what once was. Something entirely new. And they see it with their own eyes; fresh eyes that do not carry the weight of a past that is nothing more than a ghost. I cannot look with eyes such as theirs and, if one day I do, I will not be myself anymore.

"Good-bye, my love," I say. And it is indeed a farewell. The next time I see her, many years from now, I will be another.

After a while I smile. "Until we meet again."

The Ravisher, The Thief

Marian Womack

"Feel him. There's still a piece of him left," her mother said, taking Paloma's hand and putting it to the back of her twin brother's neck. It was still warm. But Paloma held no illusions; he had already made the jump. What remained here was a carcass: empty, useless. His soul, his essence – whatever it was that made him who he was – was out there now, orbiting a distant star in a faraway universe, in a new home that wasn't dying as Earth was dying. If one chose to believe the parrot chants of the new believers. Here, now, to those who had cared for him, he was dead; they would have to bury him. So she prayed to the Raptors that he had made the jump safely, that she was wrong and he was right.

It had taken her two days to get there by foot, the lights of the city glimmering yellow and orange at her back during the one night of her journey. It was a steep climb, leaving the sea and up into the mountains.

The camp sat on a patch of brown grass, which crunched under her feet. Inside their mother's tent it smelled of cooking, of the salvaged books and papers scattered around, of old fabric. The smells were mixed up with the hot, clammy air that entered through the open flap. "Feel him", her mother had said as soon as Paloma entered, taking her hand.

Outside she could hear the birds, demented in their own tent, the kestrels, the merlins, the peregrines. She could feel their intense energy, her mind's eye sensitive to their nervous bating. Everyone knew the birds were psychic, and it was obvious to her that they had sensed her brother jumping. It was also obvious that the heresy had been too much to bear for the sacred creatures, for their displeasure was unusual; as if they did not understand, or as if they were mildly afraid. A silent and contained fear. None of their childlike, irritated shrieks. She could see it, as clearly as if she were with them in their tent: the round eyes opened, the general panting and dishevelled feathers. Her own merlin had known something was wrong days before she had: his eyes shining wildly, his plumage tousled and on point. He had been unsettled even before she got word from her mother's commune kestrel.

And now another bird had sought her out here, bringing word from the Temple itself. She unrolled the parchment for the sake of her mother, always suspicious of her mind's connection to the birds, and read out loud the words she had already known she would find there.

"They need me back. There is an embassy coming and they need me to translate."

The words hung in the air like an unwanted thing. She had no desire to stay a minute longer, and her mother knew it. Paloma felt as guilty as if she had conjured up the bird herself.

That evening she stepped out for a moment, and walked in the direction of the copse. She ended up standing among the eucalyptus trees. She didn't know what took her there, to the spot where they had enacted their endless religious arguments. *We shared a womb, but had become so distant from one another. Your eyes shone when you talked about the jump, the opportunities at a distant star for the abandoned, the disinherited. It was hard for me to keep saying that there was no evidence that any of it was true. And you disdained me in return, my belief that the Raptors would fly to another world and return with instructions on how to survive. Mother always insisted: no talking about religion; and so whenever I visited we'd both come out here for our shouting matches. They're thieves, you would say, they're feeding off us; they'll eat us up in the end. It's the etymology: look up their Latin name, you'd say. Did Mum and Dad teach you nothing? By then you were half mad, spitting, your eyes bloodshot.*

What had brought her out into the copse? Little routines

are difficult to shake off, even at such times. She rolled her herbs, lit up and inhaled deeply. In her hand she was holding the vial where the poison had been.

It was then that she saw him, in among the trees, his legs set slightly apart. One hand in the pocket of his jeans, and with the other bringing the smoke to his mouth and taking long slow drags, exactly as he did while he was here; exactly as he did while he was still alive, she could not help thinking. The twin brother she had abandoned to seek a better prospect.

Her brother's shadow turned to look at her.

It was only for one second, a moment out of time, out of reality, in which their eyes locked impossibly, either across the universe, as he hoped, or perhaps through a small rift between here and there, between life and death, like she feared. And which one of them was right?

Her brother's shadow flickered, and he was gone.

Paloma had never been summoned here before, and had never wanted to enter. The place was too much; it scared her slightly.

Among the rubble of the old civilization, the makeshift abodes, the new clay constructions, stood that monstrosity like an unwanted crown on the head of a reluctant king. The Temple was all that remained of one journey for her race that had come to a hasty end generations back. It had been called the Holy Family in those days, the *Sagrada Família*, but no one knew to what family it might refer: probably some king or other, one of those few, far too few, who had owned the resources of the planet, sending the rest of the human flock down a spiral of destruction. The building was impressive; some even said beautiful, despite its lack of avian ornamentation, but it spoke of a past world of fanciful constructions and wasteful artisanship. She had to gather her strength to set foot inside; her merlin had been left behind in her rooms, and without him she was feeling her loneliness acutely.

The Temple was now home to the Falconers. Around her many towers – more than ten surrounding the central one, a massive white cone shooting up as if it wanted to reach out as much as possible without flying – circled the many raptors that lived in the building: the merlin and the peregrine, the kestrel and the falcons – red-footed, lanner, barbary. She could also see some flying men, with their makeshift wings and their pince-nez, keeping an eye on the city.

"This way, please."

She walked in. The inside of the Temple was vast, and slightly confusing in its openness. She saw a forest of columns, all of them finishing in a profusion of what looked like carved palm leaves, all of them as high as it was possible to imagine, and judged that the builders had got it right: for a forest, of any kind, was the most sacred place on Earth, as it gave protection to all creatures. There were hundreds of people walking around, going diligently about their business or looking up in wonder: on first impression the Temple seemed a huge hollowed room, the reverse of the monstrous shape one could see from the outside; it appeared to have no chambers or corridors, no hidden alcoves. This, she would learn soon enough, was untrue, a deception created by the clever builders of the past. The noises of whistling and cajoling were deafening; everyone seemed to be manning a different bird. The man-made sounds mixed with the chirping and the shrieking and the high notes of the birds. She followed the gazes of some people she saw, overwhelmed by the immensity of the high ceilings, the concave arcs that sustained that fantasy miles up above her head, the capricious shapes that twisted and twisted, the curves, the angles, the fanciful working that kept those empty walls standing.

Were they really empty? It was true that they lacked any of the crude feathery drawings one was used to find everywhere, and that their whiteness overwhelmed you for a second; but they had a profusion of carvings and little decorative holes and windows through which the birds flew to and fro, a constant fluttering of activity, of messages, orders, requests. It was mesmerising to watch. She had read somewhere that, long ago, those little openings had been covered with glass of different colours, and that the huge sections protected now by wood had been massive opened windows as well, also covered with translucent coloured glass. She imagined then the effect might have been dazzling; for she had also read that there used to be more light in the world back then, that their star shone more brightly, was not so used up. She found herself closing her eyes for a moment, trying to imagine 'light', huge beams of it crashing through the multicoloured glass, filling up that sacred vastness. It was impossible to picture, like looking at the signs of a language one is yet to learn.

"Please, follow me." The usher was getting impatient, and Paloma wished that they allowed a moment of reflection to everyone who entered the Temple for the first time. Reluctantly, she had to admit the place's wonder.

"I've never set foot in here before," she tried.

"Hmm," was all the usher responded.

They ducked past a long line of dutiful young seminarians – all of them intent on carrying duty, a peregrine perched on their ceremonial gloves – got to a nave, and suddenly they were up one of the towers via some very narrow spiralling steps.

"You ought to be careful when you come back down; take it slowly or you may get dizzy," the usher suggested.

Paloma thanked him, trying to keep up. Eventually they came to a recess, blocked off by a door which the usher knocked at lightly, and then opened at once to an uncovered balcony-chamber, where a man in ceremonial robes was sitting at a table surrounded by kestrels of all sizes and colours, each perched on their own pole. She marvelled at their beauty, at their number, and could hardly mumble a greeting.

"Sister Paloma, it is a pleasure."

"Father Merle, it's an honour," she said, for she instantly knew who he was. He invited her to sit down, and she did as she was told.

"I trust you got our summons."

"I did. It didn't say..."

"Lake Baikal."

"Oh!" Although she had expected as much. She knew several of the old commercial languages still in use, learnt from old books, sometimes tested, ever so slightly modified. She was capable, therefore, of understanding many embassies, but Old Rus' was in very high demand, and she was one of the few who could still speak it.

Father Merle continued with what he was doing, imping the feathers of a hawk's tail, carefully cutting and adding and repairing the weaker sections while the bird stood majestically still, her eyes and her head delicately turning, slowly, to the rhythm of Father Merle's soft whistling.

"This visit is of the outmost importance to us, Sister Paloma. You know very well how it has always been, since the beginning of our times. Whatever has come to pass..."

"Has happened first in the East."

"Exactly. This Embassy could bring us cheerful tidings, or perhaps word of something... much darker."

"The end of days?"

"It has been prophesied."

She knew what he meant. Their religious belief claimed that the birds brought many kinds of messages, sometimes from other worlds, sometimes from a past where civilization had not yet dug its own tomb. She could feel her merlin alone in her room, across the large city, longing for her: the pull hurt deeply.

"I understand. I'm ready."

"You will be allowed to carry your bird into the room where the talks are to be conducted, of course," he said, seemingly reading her mind.

"I thank you, Father."

"Well, well. Ah!" Father Merle rewarded the hawk with a

piece of raw meat, and whistled her back to her perch. It was beautifully done, and Paloma remembered the first three weeks with her merlin, all the tantrums and stubbornness the raptor had displayed. She belonged to the school of non-naming, out of some old-fashioned notion of not wanting to grow too fond of the animal. But how she was missing him now.

"The Embassy will land tomorrow at the port, and will arrive here at the Temple one day later. Go back home, retrieve your bird and pack your belongings to stay here with us for a few days."

"Thank you for this opportunity."

"Not at all, not at all…" Father Merle was already up, turning to attend to his birds, and she knew herself dismissed.

There was a school of thought that insisted that the merlins ought to be allowed to fly free during the first few days of manning. The bird would come back a few times a day to feed. This only worked with the little birds that were still learning to fly, and she had not done it. It was a common occurrence that a small merlin had ended up being killed by bigger birds of prey, and she could not have endured it. The merlin was not her first bird, but it was the first bird of her new life in the city. She thought now of those first few nights, willing herself to keep awake, for the manning meant that the bird himself should not be allowed to go to sleep; consoling him after each bate, softly whistling, endearing. Annotating each morsel of meat eaten, each time he flew back to the ceremonial glove. The endless patience. The solitary days, the moment when he was introduced to other humans, once he recognised her and only her as his companion, his soul-tamer. The first longish flight and the first return, freed from the jesses. And the bates, and the stubbornness, for her merlin had been his own bird, for as long as she could remember.

As soon as she entered she sensed that something was

not quite as it should be. It was the silence, thick like a lie, hanging wetly on the room. Her merlin was nowhere to be seen. She preferred living in a clay dwelling rather than a tent, but it had little holes cut through the walls for the birds to come and go. She had never felt the need to cover them, for her bird had never disappeared. Not once.

Her heart missed a beat when she heard his recognisable fluttering and chirping coming from the larger hole, the one through which the Temple was visible in the distance, and she rushed there. The view over the city was of a grey mass of rubble, the distant Temple, and the constant circling of raptors, so high up, some of them disappearing into the clouds, stepping into unreachable realms in their search for answers.

As soon as she was next to him, she knew her merlin was carrying a message. He had that look about him: piercing, suddenly alert.

"What is this?"

She unrolled the parchment.

The ravisher, the thief.

What could it possibly mean? The words had an odd flavour, of something heard long ago and forgotten. She left the parchment on the little wooden table and mechanically, still pondering its meaning, walked towards her clay snow-box, a luxury, where the precious meat was kept. She took out a rabbit's liver and walked back to the fluttering creature that was an extension of her own soul, which knew all of her deepest desires.

She could feel the bird's heart beating and started thinking at it: *where have you been, where you come from, what are you telling me*, but the bird would not look at her; her only dear friend: for her careful manning, all those nights and day of constant worry, had made them into one being. She presented the meat, and he pecked at the liver with such force that he bit her finger, and she cried as if she were a young and inexperienced falconer:

"Robin, no!"

She was at a loss for a second as to why she had called the merlin by her brother's name.

Later on, she felt the known noise in the latch as it vibrated up and down. She got up to open the door. A six-year-old child entered the little chamber, and went directly to caress the merlin's beak.

"Branwen. Where is your mother?"

"In the Lesser Temple."

Paloma sighed. Derora had developed a closeness to the new believers recently, to their empty promises. She had also started getting more and more silent and moody in the past few weeks, and Paloma had noticed she often left Branwen alone, when until not long ago she could not bear to be apart from the little boy.

"Have you eaten?"

She didn't wait for his answer, but went to the clay snow-box and retrieved the remaining meat.

"But... That's for him!" the child protested, unsure of how to react to her kindness.

"It doesn't matter, I'll buy more tomorrow. I've got myself some work," she explained, already putting a little frying pan on the fire. "But please don't tell anyone about the snow-box, it's a secret."

After eating his fill the child fell happily asleep on her chair, and she carried him carefully to her bed-corner.

The meal consisted of rabbits, cats and turnips, a veritable feast. Paloma sat between one of the ambassador's secretaries and one of Father Merle's assistants. Each had a bird perched behind him.

Paloma brooded at her plate. She instinctively wanted to put aside the best bits for her raptor who, unlike other beasts, was used to cooked meat; she had to force herself repeatedly to remember that the food was for her own pleasure, that the raptors had as much as they could possibly need. There was no reason to exercise her natural economies while living in the Temple.

"You are not hungry?" asked the secretary.

"It's delicious," she said, deliberately not answering the question. For she knew instantly what the problem was. She had been pecking at the sumptuous food all night, a meal she could have eaten only in her wildest dreams. She had not tasted cat in a long time, each acrid morsel as nutritious as the rest, and knew the meat came from a secret farm were the animals were reared for the very wealthy. She decided she would take some back for Branwen, if she could be careful enough not to be seen.

The reason for her darker mood was simple: the news had not been good. As a translator she was sworn to secrecy. She had been chosen because of her quiet, discreet nature. But the facts were alarming, and now she wondered whether she could cope with the pressure of knowing a truth that would remain hidden from the majority.

In the midst of the taiga, another hole had appeared, as black and menacing as all the others. But this one was different, so much so that news of its existence had to be taken to the Temple, the centre of the civilized world.

The birds that went into the hole never came out again.

They were used to their raptors moving between spheres, bringing messages and even in some cases small offerings: unknown plants, pieces of shiny fabric, things with actual colour on them, bright green, pink, yellow… This was the first time that one of the holes had opened into the true unknown.

The hole was slowly growing. It had been measured, and they kept an eye on it. Some thought this could be it, the blackness that had been prophesied, and that eventually would swallow them up.

After dinner, Father Merle caught up with her in a round alcove.

"Sister Paloma. I ought to thank you personally: your translation skills are all we had hoped for."

"Thank you, Father."

"Pray, tell me, how did you learn Old Rus'?"

And she recounted again the story of her Father and her Mother, and their love for old books and papers and parchments, and their idea that most things could be found within them.

"As a result, we were always behind the other children in reading the signs of rain in the *tomillares*, or finding our way through the shrublands."

They both laughed; Father Merle cut his laugh short.

"Sister Paloma, pray do not be offended by what I am about to say, for I do not doubt your professionalism, and your devotion to our belief…"

She frowned, unsure of where the older man was going with this.

"But, you see, I could not help noticing your look tonight. I just wanted to reassure you: there is no need to worry about what has been discussed in the Temple in these past few days."

"But you said it yourself, the prophesy…"

He looked at her intently, as if judging something.

"I would like to show you something. Would you follow me?"

They climbed up the same spiralling steps she had taken on her first visit to the Temple, but went higher this time, up to a tiny landing that could only be situated at the very tip of the tower. He opened a door into a small room: no balconies, only one window and that boarded up. Oddly, not a single bird in sight.

"I was hoping you would not mind leaving your merlin outside for a moment."

The request was odd, slightly tasteless; but she trusted him. She whistled a command, and the bird went to sit on a little perch outside the door.

"Thank you. And now, could I please ask you to sit here?"

He pointed at a chair in the middle of the room, where she sat. She lost sight of him for a moment, as he walked over to a cabinet behind her.

"Please, Sister Paloma, I must request that you close your eyes."

She sighed, unsure that she wanted to comply. But she was also curious. She took a second to sense her merlin outside: he was calm, collected. That convinced her there was no immediate danger, and slowly she let her lids fall over her eyes.

The dark, the hole in Siberia. Why did it all make her think of *him*?

A tear trickled down her cheek, and she was startled by its warm wetness. It was the first time she had cried over the loss of her twin brother.

"Open up, Sister."

Her mouth opened as her eyes did, and slowly they moved around, as nervously as a bird's eye would, as she took in her new surroundings. The whole room had become a painted blackboard of the known universe, with stars close and distant shining in mid-air, and slowly turning and moving, a light spectacle like no other she had seen.

"What…?"

Galaxies and supernovas and clouds of meteorites, in shining blue, projected in mid-air by a beam of light that came from behind her.

"What *is* this?" she managed at last.

"This, Sister Paloma, is our future."

"I don't understand…" But already the planets and the galaxies were zooming in and out, changing shape and direction, as Father Merle commanded the moving image directly to where he wanted to show her.

"AVA-2348, our final destination."

Paloma shivered.

"How far away is it?" she managed to mumble.

"Our astronomers are still working it out. Several hundred light years."

"But, how…?"

"Not all technology has been lost, and we've had help, from our brothers and sisters of the past."

Paloma turned to look at Father Merle.

"But I thought they were helping us to solve *this* mess..."

He smiled, ever so slightly, before saying: "This *mess*, as you call it, has no solution, my dear."

"But, how are we going to get there?"

"I think you already know that."

She didn't know what to say. Was it possible? Father Merle was one of the most powerful Falconers in Barna. Had he really gone to the other side? Had he really fallen for the sermons of the new believers? The preaching of a sect? It could not be true.

Then it hit her: this room was not difficult for the other priests to find. It was not hidden. She could not remember Father Merle even opening it with a key. Her whole body shivered at the implications: that they all knew, and they had already made a decision.

"Father Merle... What are you trying to tell me?"

"Our doctrine needs to change. We need to pass on the joyful message."

"Joyful message?"

"There is a place beyond the stars so full of wonders, so beautiful, with so much life! And it is ours!"

"Ours?" Paloma could not believe her ears.

"Well, not *ours*, exactly, only of the courageous ones."

"And what do they need to do, these people?"

"It's very simple, really. I'm sure you've heard about it."

"Drink the potion?"

"That's exactly it!" He was smiling now, a wide fixed smile, as though he were a teacher and she a particularly apt pupil. "I like you, Paloma. You are young, and clever, and a good believer. Here!" He handed her a vial. She held it in her hand, unsure of what to do with such thing.

"I... Thank you, Father Merle," she managed to mumble. She had sensed her raptor's nerves, and was eager to get out.

"Sister Paloma!" he cried, as she was about to leave. "Do

you own a clay snow-box? For your bird's meat?"

She managed a nod.

"It is better to keep it there. For the time being, until you're ready, that is." He smiled, and this time his lips were curving madly, and his eyes shone exactly like Robin's had, and she had to fight the tears, force them to hang a second longer by sheer will. "It is very precious, you know." he added.

"I will... Thank you, Father."

Once she was outside the room, her merlin went to her arm and she found herself hurrying down the steps without looking back, down that same spiralling narrow staircase that ought to be taken slowly. The hurried descent eventually made her sick and dizzy, and she had to use one of its openings, high over the city, to let out a stream of vomit.

She was recuperating when she felt it with a jolt: *The ravisher, the thief.* It was her brother the message had reminded her of. *The ravisher, the thief.* It sounded exactly like one of the things he would say in their endless religious arguments. *Look up their Latin name, would you?* he had said. *Did Mum and Dad teach you nothing?* The word she was meant to check was Raptor, of course. At those times, when he was more difficult to handle, when he was lost in his grandiose schemes and stopped making sense... At those times when she had not listened to him. Her mother had asked her back to visit, and she had not always gone. *The ravisher, the thief.* What had he been trying to tell her?

From her window she could see the city at her feet. Little yellow lights flickered here and there, and bigger fires looked like enormous circles of light, newborn stars around which other planets gravitated.

She wondered what would happen if she went to one of the fires and dropped the vial into it. Would there be an explosion? She was considering the damned thing, clasped in her hand, and it struck her how beautiful it looked, it seemed to contain all the colours she imagined the world ought to have, dancing in the viscous liquid.

She could not think, it was unbearably hot and her bird was getting uneasy. She left the vial inside the snow-box, put on her walking glove, whistled the merlin up onto it, and they left the room.

They walked down to the sea together, the bird on her arm, only going for short flights to return hastily. Eventually they turned back and crossed the city again, the endless thoroughfares, straight lines dreamed by the architects of past days. Some constructions remained from those times, huge and ugly and covered in dirt and weeds and rubble. Standing on every possible corner there were people shouting their goods for barter and the continual aviary-related business, both legal and illegal,.

They reached the beginning of the climb back to her mother's camp, and she had the sinking feeling that she would never go back there. She thought of the vial then, and started walking back home. She had made a decision. After all, she had nothing to lose, and she should have listened, really. She thought that she now understood Robin better.

Merlin was starting to feel a tad heavy on her arm, too nervy, and she petted him for a bit. At last she whistled him to go for a longer fly, she thought he needed one. She continued walking, knowing that he would be back to find her later.

But he had decided to take his time, it seemed, and Paloma started to get worried.

At last she saw him; she could recognise him at a great distance, even in a sky heavy with dozens of birds. It was him, and her heart leaped a little; it was him, and he was carrying something back.

As her merlin approached her, he dropped his present at her, and she caught it in mid-air, that horrid offering.

It was the vial, and it was empty.

Paloma started panting: the implications of this empty object, useless in her hand.

The bird fluttered around her, pecking madly; for she

had not offered her gloved arm, and the bird wanted to rest on it. But what she thought for a moment was that he was trying to attack her. She was thinking something else, another heresy, equally horrible.

She set off running towards her house as fast as her legs would carry her, as fast as it was humanly possible to do so, wishing that she could fly.

Heinrich Himmler in the Barcelona Hallucination Cell

Ian Watson

The torment cell disorients Reichsführer Heinrich Himmler, therefore he perches himself on the tilted black bench next to General Sagardía.

Sagardía has been with Himmler since the Reichsführer arrived in Spain four days earlier to prepare the way for Hitler's meeting with Generalísimo Franco – which went badly today, according to a phone call. Sagardía was in the Spanish delegation to Germany the previous month. At the start of the civil war he was hauled from his cosy 'retirement' in France; 'My country needs me.' A murderous mediocrity.

The bench tilts at an angle of 20 degrees so that a prisoner can't sleep without rolling off. Nor can the prisoner sleep upon the concrete floor, since bricks jut up harshly at random. Exhausting!

Nor, due to the awkward bricks, can a person pace the cell. Himmler has managed to plant his black boots flatly between two bricks to steady himself – his coordination isn't as good as it might be.

What a Jew of a day this has turned out to be. The journey to Montserrat monastery to take possession of the Holy Grail, a total failure. His briefcase stolen from the Ritz Hotel. The Führer, infuriated by Franco's pigheadedness.

The damnable news that the briefcase went missing came towards the end of the reception given by Dr Jaeger, the German Consul General, in his residence. Which was

Ian Watson

prior to the scheduled dinner at the Rathaus – called the *Casa Major* or something, Barcelona's town hall in Plaza some saint or other. That theft certainly put die Katze im Taubenschlag, the cat in the pigeon loft, as regards the stupid pigeonhead Spanish police! For sure the reception was soured.

Painted on one wall of the cell is an eye-dazing chequerboard. Spots little and large orbit around, red, white, black.

That chequerboard draws your gaze to it nauseatingly. Like a Kandinsky in the degenerate art exhibition Goebbels commissioned in '37, all those unGerman works displaying mental disease...

Over dinner in the Rathaus, the Mayor of Barcelona described these cells of degenerate art so as to distract attention from a succession of police officers reporting to munching General Orgaz about how the Ritz and the whole city were now being shaken vigorously, in vain, in pursuit of the missing briefcase. So here's the jowly, fat-faced Captain General of Catalonia within the crowded cell, suffering consequences.

What's the Mayor of Barcelona's wretched name again? Miguel... *Mateu*. So he's here too, in the cell. Even though these Spaniards dined so late, Himmler promptly insisted on a visit to the cells. Partly this was to punish his hosts, but also out of fascination –it's important to research new information encountered in life, personally if possible, meticulously and exhaustively. Maybe the Gestapo can learn a new trick.

The German Consul, Dr Jaeger, is here too in the cell for his sins. Only after the theft was reported did the Consul confess to Himmler that the staff of the Ritz notoriously 'used to be' infiltrated with spies – waiters trying to eavesdrop on important discussions, snooping chambermaids.

Mind you, prior to Himmler's trip Canaris idly mentioned one supposed piece of Ritz history: when the exiled Jew Bolshevik Trotsky was icepicked in Mexico a couple of months earlier by a Soviet agent, that selfsame Catalan Communist who murdered Trotsky worked in the Barcelona Ritz hotel at the outbreak of the Spanish Civil War.

If Canaris was to be trusted! Too fluent in English by half, and in Spanish too, is Canaris. Him with his own rival military intelligence service.

It couldn't be, could it, that Canaris has anything to do with the ingrate Franco refusing to join forces with Germany and allow the Reich a corridor through Spain to capture Gibraltar? Unthinkable! Admiral Canaris, if anybody, knows the strategic importance of the British Rock...

"Those cells use psychotechniques," the Mayor had said in English, with an American accent, at the dinner table, Gruppenführer Karl Wolff translating for Himmler's benefit.

A string quintet was playing during dinner in the 'Chronicles Room' of that Spanish Rathaus. The Prelude to *Lohengrin*, the *Siegfried Idyll*, a flute doing duty for the tiny trumpet part...

The floor of the 'Chronicles Room' was of black marble. Its walls and ceiling were murals of obscure historical happenings, painted upon expanses of gold and silver leaf.

"Art to punish and disorient prisoners," continued the Mayor. "This was how the Reds dealt with opposition while they were still in control here – though we aren't sure if Companys knew about this personally."

Companys, the President of Catalonia during the red republic, was shot by firing squad in Barcelona's castle just four days before Himmler arrived in Spain, maybe as a way of saying 'Thank You' to the Gestapo for catching that pest in Paris and handing him back.

By all means mention Companys! Another example of the generosity and support of Germany for the pipsqueak

115

Generalísimo!

Himmler's meticulous work in Madrid, buttering up Franco, was as much in vain as the hunt for the Holy Grail – or for the Ark of the Covenant in Toledo.

Come to think of it, Canaris had pointed Himmler towards Toledo as regards the Ark... The Toledo tip-off was thanks to interrogations of a rabbi in Auschwitz, an initiate in Kabbalah, Canaris had assured Himmler, so this might be credible. Except that it wasn't.

"Psychotechniques –" repeated the Mayor, while Himmler toyed with his vegetables.

General Orgiz had before him a plate of thick bloody Rossini steak, foie piled on top. Slaughtering birds and beasts for food is a crime against the natural world, although at times one has to go hunting with a rifle, smilingly on account of one's companions.

"– devised by a Republican torturer so-called artist named Alfonso Laurencic, and carried out by his depraved artisan Garrigós. We executed Laurencic over a year ago. Laurencic also designed special tight 'wardrobes' which constantly stress a prisoner – quarter of an hour in one of those could break a man... Just another of the atrocities of the red scum. Laurencic had a red beard," added Mateu.

"You still use his cells?" enquired Himmler.

The Mayor shrugged. "We restored civilisation."

"Permanent vigilance, and *repression when necessary*, is the ticket," said General Sagardía. "I'm sure you understand, Reichsführer."

Did 'permanent vigilance' include keeping an eye on the briefcase of the head of the Gestapo and of SS? These Spaniards! Noisy, hot-blooded, over-excitable lot. Their wine and their women and their cruel primitive bull fighting – one bullfight in Madrid was enough to last Himmler a lifetime. When Himmler presented the toreadors, toreros, whatever the word, with good German medals, one of the bull-killers said, "Medals are all very well for the Virgin, but what about the ears and tail?" Barbaric.

As for their pathetic agriculture, how can it be so bad when so much rain seems to fall? The agronomist in Himmler is appalled at the neglect.

Doubtless the thief broke into that suite at the Ritz after traversing several wrought-iron balconies by way of the linking ledges, making a mockery of the armed police stationed or snoozing in the corridor. Lurking crouched down on the same balcony from which earlier Himmler had saluted the multitude; awaiting any opportunity. The thief risked being spotted but it was night and no one was paying attention.

What roars of admiration had come from the crowd after lunch when Himmler saluted – which was gratifying; yet to be obliged to put on a show for these bull-killers...

Wolff apologised deeply that the SS guard within the suite absented himself briefly; once back in Germany, the man would be sent to an extermination kommando in Russia to redeem himself.

General Orgaz was blaming the British Secret Service for the theft of the briefcase, presumably on the grounds that the Spanish themselves couldn't be blamed if *British* spies were involved, cream of the cream. Alternatively, the French Resistance was to blame. Yet why not another *Red* spy, someone like Trotsky's killer who cut his teeth right here? Hadn't Franco's cronies cleaned all the stables of red scum completely yet?

The briefcase held documents about the agreements Himmler had negotiated in Madrid between the Spanish secret police and the Gestapo; also a report about the German community in Catalonia, courtesy of Dr Jaeger – and, on top of those, priceless ancient plans of the monastery at Montserrat, its secret catacombs and tunnels where the Grail might be kept hidden. That seat of learning published its first book at the end of the 15th century, yet it possessed in its library *no copy* of Wolfram von Eschenbach's *Parzifal* – or so claimed the junior monk spokesman, Andreu or somebody, because the abbot himself refused to meet with Himmler.

One young monk: the *only* German speaker in the whole learnèd monastery – was that credible? The occult plans of tunnels proved useless.

No copy of the great *Parzifal* poem was literally incredible when Wagner's *Parsifal* received its first authorised performance beyond Bayreuth in Barcelona *precisely due* to proximity to Montserrat – which should be the Montsalvat of the opera, home of the Grail. Himmler had been driven past the Lyceum opera house or whatever it was called on his way to the Ritz through swastika-hung streets. After the time-wasting charming folk dances and displays of gymnastics by young people.

"Exhaustion, plus hallucinatory art to derange the prisoner," said Mateu.

"I wish to see those cells," Himmler declared.

Orgaz wiped his lips with his linen napkin. "We'll take you there tomorrow morning. Mañana. The Vallmájor checa, I think."

"*Cheka* – are you referring to Lenin's political police?" Vicious, sadistic murderers...

"Alfonso Laurencic designed the system of local lock-ups for interrogation and punishment based on the Russian Checa model."

"I want to see those cells *now*. Because I shall fly back to Berlin as soon as possible tomorrow morning."

Orgaz was astonished. "*Right now?* But I believe the dessert will be raspberry and peach Melba... created by Escoffier himself, the Emperor of Chefs as your very own Kaiser said. The inspirer of the Ritz hotels!"

Himmler smiled very thinly.

"The Melba might be exceptional."

Likewise, the security at the Ritz...

"Even," added Orgaz, "legendary." Was the Captain General snidely implying something about Himmler's quest earlier today? If so, how infuriating. Due to the curse of doctrinaire fanatical Catholicism, these people had no idea of deep occult truths. As a reincarnation of the first pan-Germanic king, Heinrich the Fowler, Himmler knew much better.

"Scoff your dessert, then. I insist we leave within thirty minutes." Presumably Wolff translated a less insulting word than 'scoff', *hinunterschlingen*.

"At least take a coffee first, Reichsführer. Best Brazilian beans, by way of Lisbon, so I hear."

The Spanish might well misinterpret Himmler's thin smile as cordiality. He learned long ago not to give obvious vent to anger; better to store up such feelings for subsequent vengeance. Yet, above all, he must not be taken for a fool.

Resigning himself to some delay, he insisted, "As allies, we will *all* go together to see the hallucination cells."

Allies! As regards Gestapo liaison with Franco's police, yes. This cost the Spanish nothing to agree to, and benefited them. Among the thousands of Germans living in Spain, refugee enemies of the Reich lurked amongst the businessmen, a potential fifth column of foreigners. As to joining with Germany in the war, Himmler could still hear Franco's squeaky voice whining at his Pardo Palace outside Madrid about bad harvests, bad transport for German food aid, Spain's greed for more of north Africa. Here in Barcelona, Himmler had handed over thousands of Reichsmarks in aid to flood victims. Good old Uncle Deutschland, much obliged. Spain, willing to do what in return?

The chequerboard, like a vertical maze for mice, the coloured circles, the wavy lines disorient Himmler. The light is too bright; the lines swim; the black and white squares pulse in and out. This has been a long day. He begins to hallucinate or slip into semi-dreams.

"Welcome to Adventures in Art History! Your selection is Twentieth Century Nazi Era —"

A different woman's voice interrupts distantly. "Henry?

Henry from Harvard, you've become lost. You're submerged. Seek-Engine Vasari's expanding its reach, sucking in petaflops of historical detail. It's spinning out of control, attaching more and more strands to its web."

A voice in his head, coming and going. How can he understand a voice speaking English? Yet he seems to... Is this occult knowledge? Some of what the woman says is nonsense: seek-engine, petaflop...

"You should never have come to Himmler as a Viewpoint. To Göring, yes – he looted art. Or Goebbels – he was involved in the Degenerate Art exhibition. Or Rosenberg. Or the idiotic von Ribbentrop who liked French painters such as Utrillo even if Utrillo was degenerate. You should be in the Jeu de Paume in Paris, where looted art was assessed. Or at the Degenerate show in Berlin. *Better still*, you should never have impsoned as a Nazi bigwig."

Much eludes him. It's like overhearing someone talking a hundred metres away.

I don't understand. Are you the power I seek for the Reich?

Power. *Macht.* The Reich already has the Holy Spear safe in Nuremburg. The Ark of the Covenant remains elusive – a wooden chest once clad in gold, probably unclad these days. Himmler was in Toledo a couple of days ago, and his aides found nothing. He was at Montserrat today, only to be frustrated.

Yet now a voice speaks to him in his head.

"*Power,*" the woman says more clearly. "*Drawing so much power. The seek-engine may have gone A.I. It's autonomous, learning.*" None of this makes any sense. "*Learning the wrong things. Learning to be evil. Himmler and his cronies were nutty as fruitcakes. We're afraid this isn't exactly a sim any more. It's so detailed that it's coalescing with past reality. Identity of indiscernibles, Leibnitz. You know about this, Henry. No, scrub that – David says the sim's coalescing with an actual alternative reality within Many Worlds, not very 'alternative' at all, leastways at this time period, 1940, almost identical. David's in my ear. He's saying our assumption that time retains the same pace, same rate of progress from past to future, in Many Worlds is wrong. Henry, you gotta do something dramatically out of kilter to break the, well, congruence – I nearly said enchantment. The seek-engine is eating up our processing power. Wait, David's saying No Don't Not Yet. This is a kind of time travel, he says. Fuck that, David, this is too dangerous. Henry, does your Himmler have a pistol? Walther 25 calibre, say, specially sewn pocket in his trousers, just like his beloved Führer?"*

Himmler's fingertips grope. Pistol, yes.

The power of degenerate art to corrupt a visionary German... A wave of nausea sweeps through him, but he doesn't vomit his vegetables. Time seems to have stopped. The clock inset in the wall isn't moving its hands. Clever idea, that clock – it gains four hours in every twenty-four, to disorient a prisoner further. Now the clock seems stuck.

"The cell is a psychotrap. The way it was designed, the way it was painted. Henry, you're experiencing psychotic dissolution. Cause Heinrich to pull his pistol and shoot the others in the cell. Fegg off, David – you said the sim's resonating with an alternative reality, not with our own reality in the past. We'll break the link, disrupt the sim, collapse it like cards, resetting the seek-engine. What does it matter if the alt-reality diverges? That's the disruption we need. And we'll rescue Henry, too."

The black and white squares throb. The lines on the wall oscillate. Red and yellow discs dance. Himmler's fingers wriggle. Suffocating, in the cell. Heavily-dressed bodies crowding it. Body odours and cologne.

"You listen to me, David, damn it! Is there any chance that the sim's resonating with our own reality in the past? What would the consequences be of Himmler apparently losing his marbles and shooting people in that cell? If he shoots Consul-General Jaeger, witnessed by the Spanish, what difference may that make? Jaeger may be replaced as a minor player and the world bumps along... But if SS Wolff stops a bullet? For Chrissake, Wolff is Himmler's Chief of Staff. He's third in command of the SS, a rival to Heydrich. He's Himmler's

peephole upon Hitler. He ends up as military commander in Italy, so it's him who negotiates the surrender with Dulles. Yet he stays a mystery man, even after he starts appearing on post-war TV, authenticating the Hitler Diaries, whatever. Who replaces such an enigma?

"Shoot the Spanish? Because they have no major roles to play? Himmler is unhappy with his visit to Spain, so he shoots two of Franco's top henchmen? Do you think he'll get away with this, escape back to Berlin? Off to a sanatorium for a few weeks to keep his head down?

"Oh yes, David, we thought it would be so safe and ring fenced and marginal if we focused first upon art history. Yet what if art is one of the primary forces in the world? A definer of reality."

Power. *Control!* He must control. In this psychotic cell he is controlled *unacceptably*. Why should he even try to please any of his Spanish hosts, when the reason for pleasing them vanished with the failure of the Führer's meeting with Franco? He has pleased too many people in the past! Oh to be back home in Germany. Why should this odious Spanish experience be happening to him?

"Himmler shooting his own Chief of Staff might have the big impact we need?"

He has to release himself, break the frozen ice of the moment. How better than with a bullet? Or several?

"We truly daren't wait much longer, David. Truly so?"

To shoot or not to shoot? Blood, even brains, might spatter his uniform, his face, his glasses. If only the Führer were here to command him, *Shoot, my faithful Heini!* Then to reward him for doing the right thing, with *Well done, my faithful Heini.* No, that's his wife's voice, a woman's voice.

Only once in two thousand years is an Adolf Hitler born! A more-than-man who can command instantly, choosing the true path instinctively. Heini is not himself a Führer. Head of the SS, oh yes. Head of the Gestapo, indeed. But not the more-than-human Godhead of Germany, not a Hitler.

He wavers. The psychocell fluctuates, as though underwater. Have his glasses steamed over? The claustrophobia. The stifling.

"Leave it up to Himmler who he shoots? Because he isn't a puppet but a person? What's with this humanising of Himmler? You of all people, David! Can't you take the responsibility of deciding? And then we won't be interfering quite so much? Is that it?

"Really, we have less than a minute? Before this flux loses fluidity? Before we lose our power to act?

"So there's no authority higher than me. Under protest, then...

"Henry –! Heini –! How many people have you caused to be killed? How many more do you want killed to cleanse the Reich? You can kill a couple personally! Go ahead, this isn't so hard, Reichsführer. Then you'll be free."

The others in the cell don't move as Himmler slides the pistol from the pocket inside of his pocket. Yes, first shoot General Sagardía to one side of him – next, General Orgaz. Damn them for bringing him to this tormenting place which he insisted on being brought to.

Pull pistol, point sideways where the heart should be, squeeze trigger.

As Sagardía sags, blood spilling suddenly from his mouth and nose, the yellow lines on the wall whiplash the coloured discs and black and white squares and the dazzle of the lightbulb into a frenzied dance, spiralling inward –

"Henry? Henry?"

Sara-17-Vee-Chang eases the induction helmet from Henry-54-Kay-Patel's head, its feelers pulling loose with slight reluctance. Henry's jumpsuit-clad limbs jerk; tethers keep him where is on the couch. Very soon the spasms abate and his eyes blink open.

"Sara." Recognition. "I'm back. Quite a ride." Still ordinary, his speech.

She loosens tethers.

The viewtank, which previously showed Henry's viewpoint as if through wobbly green jelly, is now a globe of bubbly grey frogspawn, lots of tiny eyeballs with black pupils; it's in a resting state, shifting slowly around.

The spherechamber's curving wall is slim-corded with cabling. Sara-17-Vee-Chang's silver skull-ports wear data-jewels; Henry-54-Kay-Patel's ports of course await replenishing, whereupon he'll become superconscious.

No one from the Nazi Reich, except perhaps degenerate artists, could begin to guess who these slim, bald, brown-skinned beings with silver skull-ports might be, or where, or when. In fact they're in Rome, lapped by sea from the south-west. Ah, here comes David-88-Aitch-BarKohan in person.

Transhumanity has transpired rather than Overmen.

For Lluis Salvador, good guy and good guide

Dark Pages

Ian Whates

His name was Darkness, Malevolence, Spite. Born of blade and blood, he answered to all of these and more.

Awareness didn't spring upon him full-blown, but rather rose by degree, so that he could never pinpoint a specific moment that it first took shape, when a rudimentary thirst for violence and hunger for mayhem reached a tipping point and became something more. It had been a process, not a revelation.

Initially he didn't have to look far to slake the thirst that had roused him, for the tale he inhabited was a lusty one, full of dark deeds and even darker endings for the perpetrators. Soon, however, this was not enough. It dawned on him that the deaths, the gorings, the bloody battles, were the *same* deaths, the same gorings and the same bloody battles. He was caught in a cycle that endlessly repeated and its taste, which had once seemed so fresh and exhilarating, had grown stale. The certainty grew that there had to be more than this, that there were other stories than the one he knew. Yet, strive as he might, a means of accessing them eluded him.

Until...

A day came when his world was uprooted, lifted, turned, and broken open, its pages riffled through by the hand of some unimaginable god; only for a moment, before being replaced, returned to its normal state as if the disturbance had never been.

This experience opened new concepts and showed him the way. He was strong enough, *hungry* enough. He had outgrown the tale that shackled him and was ready to venture beyond. That night, when darkness was at its peak, he did.

Breaking free of page and binding, he stepped forth into the realm of the gods. A blacker shade of night, he stood, he swirled, he broiled, taking precious seconds to get his bearings, to make sense of this new and alien realm.

His world, his home, the only existence he had ever known, stood sentry-straight, bracketed by others, and beyond them stood more: hundreds, *thousands* more. Rank upon rank, row upon row of them, climbing up the wall one atop the other and stretching away into the distance. He flowed along their length, sensing within their pages others like him. No! *Not* like him. These were rudimentary, primitive things, mere glimmerings that were still groping in the dark and remained a long way short of any level of consciousness. He dismissed them and moved on, hunger his guide and his goad.

He continued forward, round twist and turn, and ahead of him… light.

More cautious now, smoke drifting across the floor, he extended his form and approached the illumination, coming up against a solid but transparent barrier. Lights, both inside and beyond. Stone pillars guarding what appeared to be a gateway into a wider world.

Outside, grey tiled paving, a line of brightly coloured chariots, sparse trees, and directly facing him a solid bank of white-stone buildings, implausibly tall and crowded together, shoulder-to-shoulder, conjoined, even as the world he had emerged from was with its neighbours. In one such, beneath an iron balcony, stood a hostelry or perhaps refectory, indecipherable white script above its doors presumably defining its purpose.

All of this he took in at a glance, his focus centred on a more immediate presence. Leaning against one of the pillars that bracketed the doorway was a figure, its back to him, facing out into the world beyond. Was this the same god that had shown him the route out of his narrow world? No, not the same, and no god either, he judged. A guardian perhaps, stationed to keep the likes of him in place? If so, a poor one, because it was paying no attention to its charge and seemed to lack sufficient co-ordination to even stand unaided, judging by the way it slouched against the pillar.

He observed the creature, the *man*, for a protracted moment, noting the frequent rise and fall of one limb between its other hand and face. Was it *feeding*?

The thought reminded him of his own gnawing hunger and he suddenly saw the creature in a new light. Food.

The transparent barrier stood between them but he had conquered the challenge of escaping his home realm, surely he could overcome this. He gathered himself and strained... and after the briefest resistance flowed through. In an instant he was upon the guardian, engulfing, crushing, consuming.

Whatever the man had been holding fell to the ground, worm-like contents spilling across the strange grey-white tiles. His hapless victim attempted to emit a scream, but little sound escaped and all the act did was allow him easy access to its mouth, its nostrils its eyes...

Bones cracked, organs ruptured, and he absorbed it all: the blood, the energy, the substance. In seconds it was over. The man was gone with just the spilled worms and discarded carton to mark that it had ever been here.

Darkness paused, savouring this new world, ready to explore, ready to feed... And yet something held him in place. Before he could fully comprehend, the compelling grip tightened and started to pull at him. He was drawn back past the pillars, up to and then through the ineffectual transparent barrier. With gathering speed he rolled past the thousands of worlds with their nascent consciousness until he reached his own. Relentless, irresistible, the force drew him back to where it had all started and forced him within.

And here he would remain; bound, sated...

For now.

Children Of The Black Lady

Virginia Pérez De La Puente

Perched like a cat on the stone railing, anyone could've taken him for a gargoyle. That is, if someone were looking and could see in the darkness. But in the gloom barely diminished by the electric lights, the only one who wasn't blind was Marc.

The Cathedral's spire poked the sky with the crucifix crowning its slender outline. Nearby rose the octagonal towers of *Santa María del Mar*, their Gothic purity tainted by the Agbar Tower's phallic shape thrusting against the skyline. Behind, the lights died as they kissed the Tibidabo's slope, the mountains of Collserola, the endless black line of the Mediterranean.

Barcelona's roofs were deserted. That in itself was a miracle he would have been grateful for if he didn't know *what* inhabited the Crucified's tabernacles. He gave a scornful grin nobody saw.

"At least you still believe in something," he muttered.

Only the distant traffic and the saltpetre-laden breeze answered. He grimaced: two years and he wasn't yet used to solitude. Laia's absence still stung.

His attention was drawn by a moan. Marc stooped over the alley twisting a hundred feet below. Anyone who saw him would have been horrified, waiting to see him fall and smash into the floor. Anyone who mistook the man crouched on the belfry as someone human enough to lose his balance.

A man had cornered a woman below the sign "*Carrer D'Hèrcules*". From high above, Marc could see her terrified face, how her eyes darted, looking for help as the man placed a hand where she hadn't consented.

Marc hesitated. That wasn't his battle. He had another, more important war to fight. But...

But that was why Marc fought alone. He stepped over the railing and dove into the air.

He landed behind the man, who clung to the woman and whispered promises Marc wished he couldn't hear. She was gathering the breath to yell something that emerged as a whimper when the man punched her belly, causing her to collapse. Marc gave him a friendly tap on the shoulder.

"Where did you learn to woo them, dude? On a YouTube tutorial?"

"Sod off, goth," the man growled, unbuttoning his belt.

"You know," Marc went on, "the Internet is full of crap, really."

He didn't even have to use his Soul to lift the man and shake him. The man kicked in the air like a frightened cockroach, emitting a rat's shriek.

"When they say no, it means *no*," Marc whispered, and slammed the man against the wall until his body went limp and slid to the floor.

A muffled moan drew his attention back to the woman. She was curled up in the corner, hugging herself, crying, her aged features contorted in agony. She was injured. Badly.

And Marc knew her.

"Anna," he exclaimed. His eyes fell over the handle of the knife buried in her abdomen. Damn. "Anna," he said softly, "Anna, it's Marc."

The Keeper's eyelids fluttered. She wasn't dead; not yet. The woman's eyes searched the nothingness but didn't seem able to find the man who had been like a son to her.

"Marc," she whined. "Marc. I was looking for you, but I didn't know where..."

"You were looking...?" he repeated. "Now? Why?"

"They wanted her Soul. Your mother's. But she refused to give it to me when they killed her", she whispered. "I've lost it. I don't have it."

Anna gazed at him with unfocused eyes, grasping the knife embedded in her stomach.

"They want her Bloodline. Now they've lost Valèria's..." Anna grasped his arm. "They want your Soul, Marc." She choked on his name.

Anna was dead even as she uttered the last syllable.

"I knew you wouldn't resist the chance to play hero, Warrior," laughed a voice. "To make you leave your hideout, one only needs to show you a helpless lump, uh?"

Marc blinked. *Warrior.* He slowly turned around, and his gaze settled on the man he'd just beaten the shit out of. That man was no man. And, by his side...

There were seven Spawns. Watching him.

Oh.

"Francesc wants to see you, Warrior. And he thought you wouldn't respond to an e-mail invitation."

Marc bit back a silent oath, cursing himself in twenty languages for being so sloppy.

"Indeed?" He raised an eyebrow. "I didn't know you Spawns engaged in diplomacy, but I have bad news: I cannot negotiate a truce. I'm a deserter."

"I may've been unclear." The Spawn pointed at Marc's chest. "Francesc doesn't want to see *you*: he wants to see your Soul."

A shiver scaled his back with ice claws. His *Soul?* His Soul was him, his Bloodline, the Source. *They want your Soul, Warrior.* His Soul was too important to allow the Spawns going near it.

Not to say that to see his Soul they needed to kill him.

The shiver dissipated, and Marc smiled; fortunately, in his book, seven to one was still a good bet.

"Pass," he answered, invoking the two knives hooked in his belt and making them leap to his hands. "And I'd never give Francesc my e-mail. I bet he's a compulsive spammer."

He jumped head first, his knives seeking their seven throats. The first Spawn fell without a sound; the second one stammered a bloody bubble before he collapsed. The third ducked and dodged a blade but the other stabbed his neck. Marc yanked the knife out and turned to the fake human, opening to the Source for the power to crush him into oblivion.

Nothing answered his call.

The Source wasn't there. Where usually he felt a hot spot lightening his chest and warming his entire body, there was only a black, empty hole. The knife slipped from his fingers and jangled on the floor; air solidified in his throat while he struggled to breathe. Without the Source, without his Bloodline, he had nothing. He *was* nothing.

Marc heard the shot as a distant creak. His legs gave way under him and his knees crashed against the cobblestones. He felt weak; he felt... human.

"So it is true,", the Spawn said. "You've lost it too. Not *now!*" he hissed. Marc raised his head and saw him tear the knife out of other Spawn's hand. "We can't kill him! Don't you see his Keeper isn't here, you wanker?"

His Keeper. Marc looked down to the blood-soaked fingers grasping his flank. He didn't feel pain; his body was numb.

"Laia," he muttered. Laia was always there. Laia was what hurt the most.

"... need his Keeper."

Marc gritted his teeth when a stabbing pain pierced his guts. He started to feel the fear's tickling. *They want your Soul.*

He had to get out of there.

Focus, he ordered himself. He was injured, disarmed and kneeling before four enemies. His hand searched his chest. He could only sense the dull, weakened gleam of his own Soul, drained after the jump from the tower and the brief fight. He barely had the energy to keep breathing. *Well, the worst that can happen is that I kill myself.* Or it could be the best.

He opened the warm core and forced it to expand, in concentric waves of blistering heat and blinding light, towards the Spawns.

And then his Soul exhausted.

Marc fell forwards and managed to plant his hands before him as he hit the ground. His breath came out in wheezing gasps, piercing his abdomen. One step away lay a heap of charred bones due to become a mystifying headache for some poor cop. In the narrow alley he could only hear his own rasping, cawing breath, and silence.

"Okay," he murmured. "Okay. Out. Now."

Grabbing the wound to keep his innards inside his body, Marc crawled to the corner and up a stone stairway, climbing in a pointed arc. He knocked once on the Gothic temple's door before he passed out in a growing puddle of his own blood.

The first thing he saw was the white rectangle of a clerical collar. Then, the hieratic face of a saint glowering at him. He blinked when the flicking candles' flames jigged before his eyes, trying to return him to unconsciousness. Pain swiped his gut; he wanted to shriek, but just managed to turn his head in time to throw up without suffocating.

"Stay still," someone grunted impatiently. "You're gonna ruin my embroidery. And then you're gonna cry because you can no longer rock a bikini."

Marc looked up, feeling dizzy. His mouth tasted as if a frog had died inside. Three years ago. Of an infectious disease.

"I never wear bikini," he spluttered when his sight focused on the face of the man gripping a curved, bloody needle.

"Sure. A naturist, eh? Be still!" the priest commanded when Marc quivered. It hurt like a thousand demons, but he was able to stay motionless until the man cut off the thread.

"Thanks, Aleix."

"Don't thank me and quit showing up at my door at obscene hours with bullets stuck in places where a bullet has no right to be," the priest grumbled. "And stop puking on my church. Do your shit and cure yourself already, man."

"Can't," Marc murmured. He couldn't reach the Source. He was *human*.

"No? I've seen you regrow your leg and put your eye back while you whined about the defeat of *el Barça*..."

"I'll have to recover the old fashioned way this time, I guess," he said, and sat up gingerly to look around. "You've taken out a fucking bullet in the middle of the fucking central nave?" he exclaimed. "Couldn't you've carried me to... to the back shop?"

"Bah, nobody comes here." Aleix looked amused. "At this hour, the back shop is like a nightclub."

Marc grimaced and tried to stand up. The basilica swirled, ready to collapse and bury him under tons of stone vaults and pillars, multi-coloured glass, fake candles and coagulated prayers. The lingering aftertaste of incense squeezed the pit of his stomach.

"I'm not gonna ask who shot you, Marc," the priest said grimly while Marc looked for his lost composure. "I'm not sure I want to know. But I'm not dumb: I know something's up, and I know that if you insist on fighting alone you're gonna get yourself killed. You should ask your people's help. Or offer them yours."

Marc pressed the wound with a hand. The bullet had embedded in his side failing to pierce any organ, but it still hurt like a sonofabitch. And he couldn't reach the Source. Maybe the Dark Folk had found a way to disavow him. Or maybe it was the Spawns' fault.

Either way, it wasn't something he wanted to discuss with a human. No matter how many times said human had saved his life.

"You don't know what you're talking about," he mumbled tensely.

"Sure I do. Why do you think I wear this?" Aleix pointed to his clerical collar. "Because it suits me? I know about the War. And I want to fight, even if I don't have the power you have."

The Eternal War. Marc sighed. He was tired. And he

didn't feel like arguing about comparative religion with a believer.

"You don't..."

"Maybe I don't. But it feels like the end, and I don't want it to end with your death." Aleix rummaged in the pocket of his jeans and took out a blister pack. "Swallow a couple of these and sleep two days straight," he ordered. "And don't you dare screw my stitches or I swear next time I'll embroider you with a cock. A tiny one."

Marc put the painkillers in his coat, turned to the altar and looked at the statue sitting in the throne over the tabernacle. The Virgin stared back with empty eyes and an enigmatic smile carved in black wood.

"*Mística Font de l'aigua de la vida.*" Marc bent his head respectfully. The Virgin's carving kept smiling; maybe she laughed too each time she heard the mantra "This is the original statue of the *Moreneta*, the authentic Virgin of Montserrat; the one in the monastery is just a copy..."

Humans. What would they know about *authentic*.

He turned his back on her and started walking towards the door.

"Be careful, Marc. You're not the first wounded Warrior to show up the basilica lately," Aleix said, "but you're the first one to survive."

Marc froze.

"Father," he breathed, "am I the first one to come without their Keeper?"

"No Warrior would move without their Keeper. Unless they're a *really* stupid Warrior."

Marc looked up towards the voice. The woman jumped from the metal chandelier tied to the vault, flipped in the air and landed between him and the basilica's door.

"Show-off," Marc grunted.

She burst into laughter, pushing her hair aside to look at him. There was amusement in her eyes, but also something else. Sadness, perhaps. Longing. Yearning.

"Laia," he muttered. His Keeper smiled.

"Marc," she mimicked. "You're hurt."

"You know I am." He sighed. Time had treated her well: she looked as dangerous as ever, dressed in darkness with almost two score knives distributed around her body. Her golden hair was damp with sweat, tied in a half-dishevelled braid.

"I felt it," she admitted. "What was it?"

"Bullet."

"A Spawn?"

"Seven," Marc said, and rolled his eyes when she arched an eyebrow. By the Goddess, he'd missed her. Two years.

"And you couldn't create a shield," Laia muttered thoughtfully.

"No."

"Are you out of training, or just old?"

"Neither," and he smiled. "And you're older than me."

"What a gentleman, reminding me of my shame."

"You're my Keeper. You've been by my side since I was born." Marc shrugged. "You're older."

"Ass." Laia made a face. "Had I been by your side a little earlier you wouldn't wear a hole in your loin and another in your shirt."

"No; we would both be dead. They wanted my Soul, Laia." He shook his head gloomily. "They killed Anna. And my mother." And he still hadn't found the time to mourn them.

She pressed her lips together. All hint of laughter had vanished from her eyes.

"There's something going on. But you've already noticed."

"I have."

"Come back." There was no plea in her voice. Laia never begged.

"No."

"You cannot fight them alone."

"I've been doing so for two years."

"But you don't *have* to," she snapped. "You left because

you wanted to, and you won't come back because you're a jerk."

"Yes. *My* fight. *My* rules."

"I think I'll let you kids play," the priest said. "I'm going to the back shop. Marc, don't be a brat or I'll spank your arse."

"Oh boy. A priest giving me the shovel talk," Marc groaned, shaking his head, and tried again to go around Laia.

"What are you looking for, Marc?" she asked irritably, grabbing his arm to stop him leaving the church. Marc shrugged.

"Answers. Blood. To kill someone. Whatever comes first in the dictionary."

"I think they come in that order. And if you want answers, I..."

"I don't care."

"Don't you care that you can't touch the Source?"

Marc froze with his hand stretching towards the handle. He turned slowly. So she knew his connection with the Source was severed. That shouldn't really surprise him. Laia was one of the Keepers harvesting the Souls and collecting them so that living Warriors could milk the power gathered in the Source. How could she not know if the Warrior whose Soul she was responsible for had been shut out?

Laia sat silently on a bench, her gaze fixed upon the altar. She looked... worried. A mood that didn't fit with the cheerful, almost bubbly picture of her Marc had nursed for the past two years.

"What's wrong?" he asked. He didn't know if he wanted an answer.

Laia bent her head and looked at her hands.

"Why did you leave?"

Marc stiffened.

"As if you didn't know."

"Yeah. I know why you left the City," she muttered. "But I don't know why you left *me*."

Marc sighed and sat by her side.

"You've spent your life awaiting my death, Laia. When I look at you, I can't think about anything else. That you're hoping to see me die."

"That's not fair," she whispered.

"Whatever," he said bluntly. "This Warrior doesn't need a Keeper circling him like a fucking vulture."

Laia laid a hand over his cheek; Marc tried to reject the contact, but instead leaned into it. Two years. The hole of Laia's absence had never been filled by his Soul, nor the Source, nor the sweetness of his Bloodline's power.

"I would give my life for it to be otherwise," she murmured. "But you're a Warrior. I'm your Keeper. I *have* to await your death, and I *have* to take your Soul."

"I know how things are," Marc snarled, the old bitterness boiling in his stomach. "But my Soul is mine. My war is the one I choose to fight. You wanted to know why I left? There's your answer."

He stood up and strode off, pretending to examine the statues frowning in his path. Right now, he only wanted Laia to be gone. And to sleep for fourteen hours, if only he could find them somewhere.

"Anna is not the first Keeper to die," Laia said behind his back. "Nor Valèria the first Warrior. The Spawns are slaying us one at a time, Marc."

"And what difference does it make?" he gritted. "They've been doing us in since the dawn of time. And we them."

"The difference is that now the Elders have closed the Well of Souls."

Marc turned so quickly that his wound howled in pain.

"They've closed the Well...? But that's not possible," he said, stunned. So that was why he couldn't reach the Source. "Why?"

Laia chewed her lip. "I don't know."

"The Spawns wanted my Soul," he insisted, confused. "But they cannot..."

"They've discovered how to use our Souls. I think the

Spawns want the two most powerful Bloodlines of the Dark Folk: Valèria's, and Enric's." She looked up. "Yours, Marc."

He said nothing, staring at her open-mouthed.

"Marc." By the fragrant half-light of the basilica, Laia looked as frightened as he felt. "You have to see your father."

"Fuck no," he growled.

"I don't have time for this," Laia sighed. "Marc, your mother just *died*. I think your father could use the company of his only son right now."

Marc licked his lips. In truth, he'd never hated his father. He loved him. He didn't clear out from home because of some childish fight with a father that adored him; he left because he couldn't kill him.

The new leader of the Spawns, Marc. He's too powerful, too ruthless, too cruel. I cannot defeat him. But you, with the power of my Bloodline and your mother's...

Kill me, my son. Kill us both. Kill us now, before it's too late.

"Okay," he mumbled. "Okay. I'll go with you. But that doesn't mean I'm back."

"Of course not," and Laia smiled.

Aleix materialised when Marc called his name as if he'd been listening behind the sacristy door. He had hidden his jeans under a white habit, and wrestled against an ample-folded garment ready to choke him. The priest smiled at Marc's incredulous glance.

"Some of us have to work to earn a living, you know," he snorted, arranging the chasuble's creases over his shoulders. "I have to give mass."

"This late? Are you kidding me?"

"God doesn't rest. And, tonight, nor do I." Aleix winked. "It's Christmas Eve, you heathen. Midnight mass."

"At midnight?"

"Duh. Are you staying? I've nothing against two non-baptised in mass, but if you're struck by divine lightning go cry somewhere else."

"Nah, we're off."

Marc followed Laia along the aisle towards the main altar, around the presbytery and up the side stairs to the golden throne where the Virgin sat, hieratic and mute. The authentic statue... Wee. The *authentic* statue, the one some shepherds found in the mountains of Montserrat, had been lost for ages. This one, copy or not, was eight or nine centuries old at best; whereas the shepherds' statue...

The statue they found in that cave was older than Christianity. Older than the goddesses whose names she'd worn. Old as the Eternal War.

Laia bent behind the throne, glancing curiously at Aleix, who had followed them struggling with his liturgical vestments. Her finger pressed the symbol carved in the wood.

"The Knot of Isis," the priest mumbled. Marc turned to him.

"You know the Lady's symbols?"

Aleix shrugged. "I'm a Catholic priest, not an uncultured punk. And I *do* know the Knot has no place in a Christian temple."

"You'd be surprised."

The wooden throne began to turn silently on its axis. Marc leant over the shadowy hole.

"You'd do better to forget this ever happened," he said quietly. Aleix nodded, and Marc jumped after Laia.

When he landed in the dark, she had already closed the passage over their heads. Marc touched his chest where his Soul flickered weakly; light bloomed in his palm, turning the darkness into penumbra.

Laia followed the tunnel sinking in the bowels of the Earth under the *basílica dels Sants Màrtirs Just i Pastor*'s foundations. And Marc followed her, swallowing the knot his memories were tying in his glottis.

He didn't remember the paintings being so vivid, or so painful. There, on the catacombs humans had never discovered while digging out archaeological remains, lay the whole of history in schematic drawings. The day the Goddess taught men how to connect their Souls with their ancestors', how to store Souls. The anointing of the first Warrior and the first Keeper, the construction of the Well of Souls. The first confrontation between the Goddess' Warriors and the Destroyer's Spawns. The beginning of the Eternal War.

He gulped when the corridor opened to the Goddess' City, still called *Barkeno* by its inhabitants.

The huge cavern rose five storeys high, the roof's dome lost in the darkness; only the stalactites shining with moisture emerged from the shadows. The square the stalagmites encircled was illuminated by the golden light of a thousand oil lamps. Ghostly faces, enlarged pitch-black pupils denied the kiss of the sun; some turned to them, some greeted them, others ignored them. None seemed concerned by the fact that, above them, the world had lived millennia unaware of their existence.

"Your father must be in the Sanctuary," Laia said, dragging him into the labyrinth of corridors that honeycombed the side of the cavern.

The Elders' Sanctuary was entombed so deeply that the cold gave way to scalding heat. The ventilation system couldn't erase the faint sulphuric scent; the air was thick; the lack of lamps turned the murk into a living, hungry beast.

Marc was a Warrior. He'd never descended to the Sanctuary, and he couldn't hide his awe at the rounded arches, the supporting columns, the filigreed ornaments, the stylized statues watching silently from their gates. Laia, on the other hand, was a Keeper; she didn't even spare a glance at the façade before pushing Marc into the shrine.

What Marc saw in the Sanctuary would be the nightmare that poisoned his dreams for the rest of his life. His heart beat wildly as he sought to peer through the darkness, a deafening roar pounding in his ears. Nothing could hide the stench of blood: viscous, metallic and full of bad omens.

The whole floor was covered with corpses.

"Goddess," Laia breathed, but Marc couldn't talk. Bile rose in his throat. He fought back vomit, blood and fear, while he glanced around at bodies dismembered, slit open, gutted, beheaded. The roar in his ears didn't cover up the slow dripping of blood on the drenched floor.

He started running when he recognised the body hanging like meat on a slaughterhouse over the circular slab closing the Well of Souls.

"No," he moaned. "No, no, no..." He dropped to the floor in front of his father's corpse, ignoring the blood soaking his jeans and caressing his sire's skin with gooey fingers. He gazed at the exsanguinated face, the blind eyes, the bloody smile slit into his throat, the arms tied to the wall as a cruel mockery of the Crucified in the church above. He couldn't think. He could only deny what his senses reported. *No, no, no,* the word stuck to his tongue like a leech.

Laia squeezed his shoulder until the roaring died. Then, Marc heard it.

A whimper.

At Enric's feet lay a man. It took Marc a second to realise he was alive; he gave a surprised cry when the man turned his face and he saw the pain-contorted features of his father's Keeper. As Anna, he had a knife buried in his guts.

It might even be the same knife that sliced Enric's neck while he hanged helpless from two hooks.

"Xavier."

The Keeper turned an unfocused, feverish gaze.

"Dead. All of them, dead, all dead..." he crooned deliriously.

"What happened?" Laia hushed.

"The Elders refused to open the Well," he explained weakly. "All dead."

"Xavier," Marc demanded. "Who killed my father?"

The Keeper closed his eyes.

"I did."

Marc didn't even feel anger. His mind was numb, his Soul anaesthetised. A tear detached from Xavier's eyelashes digging a furrow on his bloodstained cheek.

"They came for the Warlord's Soul. Enric asked me to kill him. How stupid," he smiled sadly. "He wanted to pretend he didn't give it to me. And they killed *me*." His father's Keeper showed a blood-tainted smile.

"But I have it," he whispered. "I couldn't put it into the Well; it's closed." His hand hovered over the illegible symbol engraved on the slab's surface. "But I kept it for you, Marc."

"Marc." Laia's voice rang like a warning. He turned.

Truth be told, he didn't feel surprised to see the ten men blocking the temple's entrance; but he'd been so engrossed in his shock he hadn't even considered the Spawns could still be there. He stood up, barely controlling the fury boiling in his stomach.

"Francesc, isn't it?" he guessed. One of the Spawns nodded. "I can't say I'm pleased to meet you, but I won't deny I was curious."

"Same here. Not every day I find a Warrior connected with the two oldest Bloodlines of the Dark People. Or he will be, when the Well's open."

"You knew the path to the City?"

"Keepers are weak." The Spawn walked casually towards them. "And you... you're predictable, Warrior. Show you a helpless guy," he pointed at Xavier, "and you go berserk."

By the Goddess, he *wanted* to go berserk. Not only had that utter piece of shit terrorised the Dark Folk, infesting their dreams with nightmares, because of him, his parents were dead. Because of him, Marc had left them without a final farewell.

Francesc bent over the dying Keeper.

"Give it to me," he commanded softly. "Give me the Warlord's Soul, Keeper."

Xavier blinked at the Spawns' leader.

"No," he whispered, and before Francesc had time to react the Keeper uprooted the knife from his guts and stabbed his own jugular. And he still had time to slice his throat before his fingers, drained of their strength, dropped the blade on the floor.

Laia let out a horrified gasp that Marc mimicked without realizing. However, Francesc just shrugged and turned to face them.

"You're smart enough to know that now it's your Soul I'm interested in." His smile was that of a predator smelling blood. "Are you going berserk already, Warrior?"

Yes. Oh, *yes*. All the rage he had repressed flared through Marc's being, flooding his mind and taking control of his body. His hands flew to his knives and, disregarding his brain's protest and his body's wound, he leaped towards the Spawns.

His body, his Soul and his wrath dealt with the fight without his mind's help. His world narrowed to a black and grey, red and white blur formed of anger, steel, blood and power. His arms drew silvery arches releasing bloody ribbons from the Spawns' bodies, his Soul scorched skin, broke bones, ripped open organs. He was aware of Laia by his side, bleeding Francesc's men with her gleaming daggers; but Marc could only see ire, and blood, and the overwhelming need to destroy these bastards and spread their remains across the temple floor.

He only stopped when a blow to his chest sent him stumbling. When he glanced down, his eyes fell upon the handle of a knife buried between his ribs.

Oh.

He tripped and collapsed backwards, his back hitting the stone covering the Well.

"You're an idiot, Warrior."

Francesc stopped by his side with a smirk, grabbing Laia's arm; she twisted uselessly to escape until the Spawn shoved her to the floor.

"Now, give your Soul to your Keeper."

Marc didn't feel any pain; he was too astonished to sense it. For some reason, when he looked up to Laia he saw instead Aleix's last glance.

And then he understood.

The priest had noted the Goddess's Knot, the opening of the path to Barkino. So simple. So *stupid*. The symbol closing the Well was an unfinished Knot.

"Marc," Laia whispered. "Don't do it."

He couldn't think clearly. He only knew that he needed power to smash those mongrels. His hand over his chest, he soaked his fingers in blood and, stretching his arm, traced a red line over the broken symbol.

The stone didn't move. The floor didn't shake. There was no light, no sound. But the energy sprang from the Well with the strength of a tidal wave, and fell on him so powerfully his body arched over the stone, unable to absorb so much power, so many Souls. His throat released a silent howl while his body quivered in an agonizing dance.

The world sank under his feet and cracked over his head. Heat spread throughout his body, dissolving his muscles, boiling his blood, splintering his bones. It hurt. By the Goddess, how it hurt. Hands, and hundreds of voices whispering *son, great-grandson, man, descendant, heir, you, Marc*. So much light, so much heat, so much pain. He screamed, and the scream took him back to the present and his body to the agony of knowing that, despite all the power of his Bloodlines, life was still draining out through the hole between his ribs.

He went limp. His heart thrummed in his throat like a broken-winged bird; he was deaf and blind. Then his eyelids opened and his eyes found Laia's tearful face.

His head was on his Keeper's lap, and she was caressing him without realising her tears were dripping over his sweat-soaked forehead.

She knew, too.

"So you finally get your wish," Marc said with an exhausted smile. "To be by my side while I die."

"I never wanted this."

"Yeah? Okay. Okay." He wanted to say more, but the world was fading. He was dying. Quickly. Damn.

He raised his hand and touched Laia's cheek.

"Don't do it," she begged for the first time.

"*Somophator*," he breathed.

He never felt how his body collapsed before he died, because his Soul was already springing from his body and spilling inside Laia's.

He felt again the blinding light, the unbearable heat, but this time they were distant, numb. *I'm dead*, he thought. He didn't feel; it was she who was feeling. And Marc smiled, because his Soul was inside Laia, and he laughed when he felt Laia's lips mimicking his smile.

"Now, give it to me, Keeper," the Spawn commanded.

"No."

She carefully deposited Marc's head on the floor and got up slowly, raising a hand and letting a minute fraction of the power gathered in her chest cast a dot of dazzling light that made the shadows back off and bathed the Sanctuary in whiteness.

"It cannot be," Francesc protested. "You're nothing more than a Keeper. You have no Bloodline."

"I have the two oldest Bloodlines. I have the Source. I *am* the Source."

"Give it to me," the Spawn demanded. Marc felt the tightness in her face when she raised an eyebrow.

"Come and get it."

For fuck's sake, woman, do you have to be so clichéd?, Marc groaned, and Laia guffawed before she opened the intangible gates holding the Source's power inside her core.

The last thing Marc heard were the Spawns' yells, the faint hissing of their bodies reduced to cinders in a second that turned the air into fire, the sweat into lava, the light into scorched blood. And the world faded to black.

The stone boulder pierced his back viciously, like a scavenger gnawing a corpse. The Universe was silent, black and empty as death. *So fitting.* A hand set aside the damp hair from his forehead with a caress soft as a kiss.

He blinked.

The flickering flame of a lonely oil lamp covered the corpses mercifully with a shroud of shadows.

"What," Marc murmured, struggling to sit up and giving in at the first attempt. There wasn't an inch of his body that didn't scream in pain.

"Hi." Laia kept caressing his forehead. She was smiling. She was crying, too. "Welcome back."

"What," Marc repeated idiotically.

Laia rolled her eyes.

"Warriors," she sighed. "You only know how to use your powers to kill."

"What. Wait, what?"

"I took your Soul," she explained patiently. "I gave it back."

"That's not possible."

Laia shrugged. "Clearly it is, because I just did it."

Marc sat up slowly, burying his head on his hands to soothe the pain splitting his skull. He had died, hadn't he? And Laia had brought him back to life.

A Keeper... Keepers were receptacles. They weren't connected to the Source, they couldn't use the Souls.

And nobody could resurrect the dead.

Marc closed his eyes and pushed aside the thoughts swirling dizzily inside his head. His father's corpse. Xavier's corpse. Valèria. The light. Francesc's sneer.

"Warlords don't cry," she teased quietly.

"No fucking way," he groaned. "I'm not going to take my father's place. I cleared out for that reason. And I fight better alone," he whined.

"Sure," she laughed. "You just proved that so nicely..."

Marc smiled and grazed her cheek with his knuckles.

"Fair point. It was my battle, but you won it."

"I'm still your Keeper, Marc," she sighed. "I still have to await your death."

"By my side?" Maybe that wasn't such an awful prospect. He rested his forehead on hers. "Okay."

Equi Maledicti

Sarah Singleton

The horse snaked out its head, drew back its lips and snapped. The boy jumped back, long, equine teeth missing his face by a whisker. The old man behind him roared and the horse snapped again, stamping flinty front hooves. Clumped locks of an iron grey mane moved over its sweat-soaked hide.

"What in the name of the gods?" the old man said. He had a broom in his hands which he brandished at the horse. Most would have backed off, but the horse retaliated, shouldering up, pushing its chest against the thick wooden spar across the stall, reaching out again to bite. Its ears, small and finely shaped, were curved like scimitars, pressed flat back, its eyes were white-rimmed. The old man could smell its heat and anger.

"They're all the same?"

The boy nodded. He had a bite mark on his upper arm already, a circle of deep indentations in his skin, turning blue and purple. The old man sucked his bottom lip. Six horses. Four mares and two stallions, fresh to Barcino, shipped from Alexandria. Each a different colour, all as beautiful as any animal he had ever seen, as though forged in the furnace of the desert from some refined and precious metal – contoured, sharp-edged, flawless, burnished. And useless – all of them. A curse lay on them – and now on him too, and most particularly, he decided, on the man who'd taken his money.

That man, Aurelius, in the early evening, was lying in the arms of a young Iberian woman in a room off a tavern just outside Barcino, under one of the seventy-eight towers punctuating the city wall. Through the thatch he could hear the soldiers' voices, hints of their gossip, the slap of their sandals. He imagined what they could see, the low roof of the tavern just one in a complex patchwork of makeshift buildings, the arteries of roads and lanes, the noisy populace of the outer city. The woman shifted beside him. Her skin smelled of sandalwood, and her hair was thick and long and fair. She came from the north, she said. He found the contrast of her pale cream skin with his own deep sun and sea tan novel and stimulating, and what with the dinner of lamb, the Iberian wine and a large sum of money, Aurelius allowed himself a rare moment of satisfaction.

He climbed off the low bed, dressed, thanked the woman and went out into the street. The city wall reared behind him. Inside, a grid of streets, stone villas and courtyards, and the forum – a miniature of Rome, a pocket of order tucked away and preserved from the depredations and disorder of the rest of the world.

Daylight had begun to fade. A slow trickle of people moved into and out of the tall city gates. Aurelius stopped at the foot of the wall, amongst piles of detritus. He leaned one hand against the stone and began to piss. The voyage had been difficult. Unexpected storms had thrown them off course. Several long hours of tumult had unsettled the horses, tethered beneath the deck in the hold. The captain had stinted on feed and they'd all lost condition. Nonetheless, when they trotted down the ramp to the quay at Barcino, necks arched, staccato-hooved, black and bay and polished chestnut, Aurelius knew it had been worth the trouble.

A blow landed on the back of his head.

Aurelius fell to his knees, still pissing. Another blow, this time glancing down to his shoulder. At first it was only shock he felt, but when a kick landed on his lower back, pain ignited in his spine. He cried out and fell forward, face landing in a slurry of rotting fish and oyster shells. Someone stamped on him, once, twice. Another kick grazed the side of his head.

He was pulled to his feet, sensing the heat and stickiness of blood and dirt on his face, a cacophony of hurt in his body. Another face now swam inches from his own. Aurelius noted the fat pouches under its eyes, the swags of flesh hanging from its jaw, narrow eyes between thick lids.

"He hasn't got the money on him," a voice said. The man staring at Aurelius sucked his lower lip.

"I want my money back tomorrow," he said. "And you can take your horses away with you. If you don't, I will kill you. And if you try and leave without paying me, I will have you killed. And I will kill the horses too. I'll cut them off at the knees, vicious fuckers. And perhaps I'll cut you off at the knees too and you can die with them. Tomorrow, yes?"

Aurelius nodded. His mind was remote, his body and all its agony far away. The men dropped him, and gave him a couple more kicks, and then it was over. They were gone.

When Aurelius opened his eyes, darkness had fallen. The city wall cut off half the sky but ahead he could see a sweep of stars. He thought he could hear the sea. He struggled to his feet. One eye was swollen shut and blood caked his hair. Clutching his arms around himself, Aurelius dragged his way back to the lodging.

The fair-haired woman emerged from her little room with another customer, sent him off, then contemplated Aurelius in all his filthy, gory glory. She wrinkled her nose, evidently not pleased to see him.

"Will you help me?" he said. "I'll make it worth your while." He felt a childish longing for sympathy, and this woman would only give it for money. She sighed and nodded, taking his arm and guiding him into the room. Aurelius half collapsed down in the bed and faint warmth left by the other man moments before.

He awoke to a quiet tavern and found the woman bathing his face with clean, perfumed water. She'd removed his tunic. Her touch was careful and gentle.

"They say you owe a lot of money," she said, her Latin fluent but accented. "They say you cheated a man in a deal for horses. The animals are dangerous. Insane."

He tried to speak, but his lips were thick and stiff.

She shrugged. "A man followed you. A foreigner. He says he might be able to help."

Aurelius blinked with his one good eye and tried to reply. She shushed, softly. "Wait till morning," she said.

When he woke again, Aurelius lay thinking for a long time. He didn't understand this claim that the horses were crazy. They had been skittish, certainly, but nothing out of the ordinary. What had happened to them? What had the old man done? The question was beside the point. He wanted his money back. Aurelius weighted up his options. First, he could return the money and relieve him of the horses. Perhaps he could take them inland, away from Barcino, and sell them to someone else, someone with less of an appetite for violence. Second, he could run off – on a ship or more discreetly, inland. However, he was well known and sooner or later this might catch up with him. Thirdly, he could bide his time, for a few hours at least. Wait and see.

It took some effort to stand up. His back hurt the most, and his shoulder. One eye had swollen closed, and his piss had blood in it, but as he moved around, the stiffness in his joints lessened. He sat outside the tavern, in the shade of the awning, and carefully ate bread and soft slices of peach. As he did so, a man approached the table. He was dark-skinned and bearded, with a long piece of pale cloth wound around his head in a turban.

They regarded each other for a few seconds. Aurelius straightened, his hand slipping to the dagger at his waist. He felt a moment's fear. This might be more trouble.

"You're the horse dealer," the visitor said.

Aurelius nodded. "Who are you?"

"I know something about your situation. I can help you."

"Who are you? And why would you do that?"

"For recompense, of course."

"How exactly would you help me?"

"I can sort out the horses. Remove the curse."

"The horses are cursed?" Aurelius snorted. "Then who cursed them? Did you?"

The man shrugged and turned away. But as he started to walk, Aurelius called out:

"Wait."

They stood on a hill, above the city. The sun beat down. Faraway, the sea glittered. Barcino lay before them, with its grid of streets and tiled roofs. Like toys, ships in the harbour carried their cargoes of wine, olive oil, silver and spice. On the summit of the hill lay several huge, pale stones, worked with spirals, but toppled and in disarray.

In his hand, the man held, on a black cord, a horse of polished bronze. Slowly it turned, and as it caught the sun the metal flashed, and then flashed again. Aurelius reached out and clasped the metal horse. As soon as he touched it, something seemed to crawl over him, and through his entrails and into his throat. The edges of the talisman bit into his palm as he squeezed it.

Aurelius opened his fingers and stared at the horse. One of the six had been this precise colour. The metal horse had elongated legs and a high, crescent neck.

"What is this? Some kind of ridiculous magic? What am I supposed to do with it?"

The man regarded him. He wasn't tall, but he looked strong; lean and tough as rope. Hard to say how old he was. Aurelius' earlier sense of unease intensified. Had he seen him before?

"The horses are ghost-ridden. Touch each on the forehead with the talisman and it'll remove the ghost."

Aurelius was sceptical. He didn't set much store in this kind of magic. He had scant respect for the gods, come to that. Nonetheless, the talisman had something about it. He had felt that much.

"How do you know this? Who are you?" Aurelius had reasons to be wary. "What do you want for it?"

"Two things. Half the money you got for the horses."

Aurelius raised his eyebrows and snorted. "Half? And what else?"

"For you to wear the metal horse. To keep wearing it. If you take it off, the ghosts will go back to the animals."

Aurelius stared at the talisman. What did he have to lose? If this worked, he could keep the money. He had no intention of handing over half. He couldn't deal with the rich old Roman in Barcino, but this purported magician? He could handle him easily enough. Kill him if necessary, after the deed.

Aurelius stood in the stables at the Roman's villa. He was shocked by the sight of the horses. They hadn't touched food or water for two days. Their coats were dull, bones prominent, the skulls in particular seeming to press through the skin, making them hollow-eyed and ghastly. They wouldn't be still, instead twitching, jumping and snapping – at the boys in the stable but also at the air. They panted and sweated, tossing their heads.

What had happened? Poison? Seeing them, Aurelius wondered if the tale of a haunting might be true. He fingered the bronze talisman, turning it over in his hand. Would it work? He hardly dared get close enough to the horses to try.

"Well?" The old man glared at him. "Do you have my money?"

Aurelius took a deep breath and stepped towards the bay horse. As it lunged towards him, he stepped to one side and stretched out, to press the talisman on the hard bone of the horse's forehead, right between the eyes. The horse shuddered. Its body seemed to ripple, from the tip of its nose, down the long spine and out of the tail. The horse's skin appeared to breathe a fine smoke that evaporated on the air. Then – instantly – the horse stilled. Its head and neck dropped down, nose to the floor, and it gave a great sigh.

They all stood and gaped – Aurelius, the old man ad the stable boys.

"What did you do?" The old man strode over to the chestnut and patted its neck. Next he ducked into the stall and ran his hand over the horse's back, and lifted up one of its hooves. He was incredulous. The horse stood calm.

Aurelius moved to the next horse, and the next. Within moments, each was cured. He tied the narrow thong and hung the talisman around his neck.

Just before sunset, Aurelius was aboard a ship heading for Rome. He had slipped away quietly, intent on avoiding the man who had given him the bronze horse. Aurelius knew the captain well. His payment for the horses had already been stowed in a bolt of silk. The sails went up, bellied in a keen breeze, and tugged the ship along the coast. The harbour and the city fell away behind them, growing small and indistinct.

The talisman felt heavy on his chest as he lay on a bench at the side of the deck, staring at the sky and the heaving stars. Slowly his body became accustomed to the motion of the ship. The sailors moved about him, tightening and coiling ropes, occasionally passing a word or two between each other.

A line of horses in the desert. Against the brilliant, shimmering, rising sun, trotting along the top of a ridge, they were indistinct dark silhouettes, almost unreal. He was lying on his belly. The ground was cold from the night.

Aurelius narrowed his eyes and counted. Six. A man rode the first and another rode the last, the others strung between. Aurelius glanced to left and right, and nodded to his own men. The horses would pass along the stony road in front.

It took many long minutes for the distance to be closed. The sound of six sets of hooves – a barely perceptible rumble at first, and then a low percussion, and then a loud clatter. Aurelius jumped down from the bank, landing on the first rider, pushing him off the horse and to the ground. Aurelius was cushioned from the impact of the fall but he heard a bone snap in the shoulder of his victim and the man cried out. In a moment, Aurelius had grabbed the thick fabric wrapped around the man's head and sliced through his throat. The man made horrible bubbling, choking noises before he lay still. Blood everywhere, soaking into the road, hot and sticky on Aurelius' hands and cuffs. He glanced over his shoulder. His men had the second rider on the ground. He shouted out as they hauled him over and hacked at his throat. The horses had shied away, but not far. Still tied together they stood and faced the carnage, ears pricked, staring and snorting.

"Get the horses." Aurelius grabbed the dead man and dragged him off the road, up and over the bank. He kicked the dust over the already drying spread of blood.

"Let's go."

He approached the first horse – the bay stallion ridden by the man whose throat he'd cut. It wore a good saddle. An ebony forelock hung over its chiselled face. Aurelius reached out for the reins but the horse reared up. For one long moment it seemed to hang over him, the flinty hooves just above his head.

Aurelius tried to spring back but his feet seemed rooted. A hoof smashed against his head and the force knocked Aurelius to the ground. The horse reared again and the descending hooves pierced his skin, splintering his ribs. Aurelius screamed at the intolerable agony of his body's breaking. The other horses were around him now, snatching at him with their teeth, stamping on his hands and limbs. His skin tore, his muscles were pulverised, the bones cracking and shattering under the weight of their hooves and heavy bodies. The horses cried out like devils, neighing and shrieking as they ripped him apart.

Aurelius woke screaming.

The sailors on the night watch stood around him, their hands on his shoulders. His throat was raw and he gasped for air, chest heaving, limbs flailing. Seeing his eyes open, the sailors stepped back. They stared at him. One made some uncivilised kind of gesture, perhaps some appeal to the gods.

"We couldn't wake you," he said. The three sailors backed away, returned to their watch but Aurelius could feel their eyes on him. He didn't sleep again that night, but stared out at the sea. Bruises covered his body and he'd broken a tooth.

The following night the dream came again and, unusually for a dream, he felt the intense agony of the horses' attack. This time, he caught a glimpse of the man he murdered sitting on the bay stallion's back, rising from the saddle, but his throat opened up, dropping sheets of blood over his front.

When he woke, hoarse from screaming, the ship's captain was sitting beside him, a dagger in his hand.

"We'll put you on shore tomorrow," he said. "You can take your money. The men say you're cursed."

Aurelius didn't answer but turned away. Only one ghost in his dream – the man he had killed. What about the other one, the man who had cried out the dying man's name as he was bludgeoned by the others? What if they hadn't finished him properly?

Aurelius remembered the terms of the deal. If he took off the talisman the curse would return to the horses. To have the old Roman in Barcino as an enemy would not suit him. He could never go back. Well, he had no choice. Aurelius reached for the bronze horse and took it off, pulling the thong over his head. He looked at it one more time, then drew back his arm and threw it up and out, over the sea. The talisman made and arc in the air, flashed once, then fell down into the back of a wave.

Aurelius felt a moment's peace but then, slowly, an unexpected weight began to build in his chest. He tried to breathe but vomited instead. Water rose in his throat and welled into his mouth and over his lips. Burning salt water. He retched and water spilled out of him, mouth and nose, over the deck, in impossible quantities. The captain stepped back. All the sailors were looking at him. Water again, sea water, pouring out of his mouth. He was on the deck of the ship but he was drowning. Aurelius heard a roaring in his ears, and the sound of hooves, and still the water came, as though he were a conduit of the Noster Mare itself.

The Dance of the Hippacotora

Claude Lalumière

Near the end of the mythic age, a young centauride fled Greece to escape the ceaseless insults of other centaurs. Her equine half resembled the donkey more than the horse, and even her human head was marred by donkey ears. She galloped tirelessly, spurred on by her need to escape from herself, which, or course, she could not do. She wended her way past Gibraltar; the sight of the Atlantic Ocean stopped her in her tracks, partly because she could not go any farther and partly because the view mesmerised her. So she settled in Iberia and found a certain peace. Nevertheless, so far from home, at times her heart ached from loneliness. At the break of dawn, she would sometimes lie in the sand and let her tears fall into the sea as she gazed at its beauty.

On one such morning, on a Mediterranean beach east of Gibraltar, one of Poseidon's bulls – a brother of the Cretan Bull, who famously sired the notorious Minotaur upon the all-shining goddess Pasiphaë after she had been turned into a mortal, as an unwilling gift to King Minos – happened to be swimming near the Iberian coast, and he caught the taste of the female centaur's tears. As they do on many males, the tears of a female acted on him like a powerful aphrodisiac. He swam to shore and seduced the centauride.

These giant, amphibian bulls possess many attributes beyond their ability to prosper equally on land and in the sea. Of interest to us now are two related characteristics: their ability to direct their genital musk toward any female they desire and thus inflame her lust, which can then only be sated by the bull himself; and the capacity to crossbreed with any species, resulting in odd chimeras scattered like seed across the world, each of them distinct from the other.

Once this particular bull had satisfied his lust, he left the impregnated centauride sleeping on the surf of the Mediterranean. Chimeras, due in part to their unusual shapes, often induce difficult labour upon their mothers, and this small, fragile centauride was not up to the challenge. She died in childbirth, having never laid eyes on her daughter, the Hippacotora: a horned biped with the head of a cow, sharp talons for feet, and a giant third eye where her left breast should be.

The Hippacotora is still among us and can often be found in Barcelona among the living statues who ply their trade on La Rambla. Alas, she is only mildly successful at separating tourists from their funds, as she lacks the grace of the other performers. Nevertheless, she is enchanted by the beauty and bustle of Barcelona and its people, and she strives to mimic the ethereal agility displayed by her fellow artists.

When she despairs at her lack of skill, she trots away from La Rambla – and from our world altogether. The Hippacotora's third eye allows her to see the paths between realities, lets her see the exact sequence of steps necessary to leap out of this universe and into a world that is nothing but an endless labyrinth delineated by impassibly tall and thick hedges.

Sometimes, others wander into this lush maze – careless drunks, dervishes who whirl too recklessly, unsuspecting sleepwalkers. When the Hippacotora finds them – for she can always smell them as soon as they step into this other realm – she sings them to sleep, to calm their fears at being stranded in a world they cannot understand, and then she eats them – clothes, bone, and all – leaving not a trace of their short presence in her personal elysium.

Invariably, she again comes to yearn for the excitement of Barcelona and La Rambla.

She always remembers the exact sequence of steps that will take her there.

There Will Be Demons

Alberto M. Caliani

I don't know how I am still alive. Call it fortune. Call it disgrace. I can hardly believe what happened twenty minutes ago. Suddenly, all the statues in Barcelona came to life. I was caught in the middle of the mayhem, near the Diocesan Archive, when the world, without warning, became the worst horror movie you can picture. Bedlam surrounded me as I ran in terror from Carrer del Bisbe to Barcelona Cathedral: winged scaly monsters diving from the sky, grasping people with knife sharpened claws, lifting the unfortunates up high before dropping them to their doom; flying dragons burning down whole streets and crowds of people running, screaming, burning, trying to escape that inferno, as if they stood a chance. I witnessed a pack of grotesque gargoyles surround a mother with her baby. They ripped the woman's neck open and eviscerated the child two seconds later. No pity. No remorse. The last thing I saw before I locked myself behind the door of the cathedral was the mosaic salamander from Park Güell opening a huge hole on an armoured carrier, pulling soldiers out of it, in a carnival of blood, limbs and guts.

This is all too much for a humble cleric.

My name is Jordi Vendrell, and I am the parish priest of Barcelona Cathedral. I have the privilege of being the keeper of the keys of this sanctuary, and here is where I am, hiding from the apocalypse. My heart pounds fit to burst as I lean against the inside of the old wooden doors of the temple for support. I survey the statues of saints, virgins and Christ warily but, to my relief, they are static – as they should be –

unlike the rest in Barcelona. I cannot avoid the chilling vision of our crucified Lord trying to escape the cross, ripping his hands from the nails, screaming in pain. The mind can be cruel, and imagination our worst enemy. I light dozens of candles, fearing the inevitable power blackout. Surely it's just a matter of time before these animated stone creatures damage the city generators, or simply kill the people who maintain them. The last thing I want right now is darkness set against the soundtrack of Barcelona's tortured populace. Oh, Lord, I need a cigarette. Damn, the pack in my pocket is less than half full. This is my only lesser vice, and nine or ten cigarettes are nowhere near enough to sustain me through the apocalypse. Well, maybe for a quick one, but I plan to survive, hidden between these walls, for as long as possible. Maybe the army will solve this crisis, who knows... Food and water won't be a problem: we have a lot of both at the sacristy, waiting to be distributed amongst the poor. If doors are strong enough to keep the creatures out of the cathedral, I will be safe here. I just don't want to imagine a horde of stone monsters breaking through them.

Oh, God, I am so scared...

I look at the sacred statues once more. Will they come alive, like the rest? The stone angels gaze at me with their dead sculpted eyes. No life in them, thank God. Why did all the statues of the city come to life and start this orgy of destruction? How many others survive to ask the same question?

A little calmer and armed with a flashlight collected from the sacristy, I walk in circles between the wood benches. I turn my head back now and then, convinced that I am being spied on from the shadows. Suddenly, the electric lights dim and finally go off. The candles' illumination depicts everything in an oppressive shade of orange. I can't help remembering the cathedral crypts, where a lot of illustrious bones rest in peace. I wonder if the strange phenomenon that animates the grotesque statues could do the same with corpses. Icy tentacles of fear caress my spine and stomach, and I feel sick. Outside, the concert of horror and destruction reigns over the uproar of explosions. There's a battle going on out there, and I cannot do anything but fall at my knees on the closest bench. I pray, pray without knowing what I am really asking of the Creator. Here I am, the scared minister of God. I keep the flashlight turned off by my side. I will need it when the candles burn down. Oh, God, help us and destroy this diabolic enemy...

"God is not here today, cleric..."

My head whips around at the voice, and I feel on the verge of a heart attack. The voice sounded rough and creaky at the same time, definitely not human. I turn the flashlight on and sweep the darkness with its beam. Suddenly, a small fire lights a lantern, next to the main altar.

"Don't be afraid, cleric... You don't need to be."

Now I can see the owner of the voice, descending the staircase and coming in my direction, holding the lantern like a night watchman. The big crucified Jesus that dominates the altarpiece seems to observe the figure from on high. I think the stone creature represents a small grotesque male. I guess him to be about two feet tall, naked except for a small loincloth, without a single hair on his whole body. His extremities, too short to be human, end in small claws; hands and feet look very similar, like those of an ape. The nails are sharp and chipped. His face has round gargoyle features, composing a creepy expression full of fangs, with pointed ears that move as he talks. But the most horrifying thing is his eyes. They remind me of the cunning gaze of a crocodile, ready to attack. The small creature continues to walk forward until he stops directly in front of me, favouring me with the most hair-rising smile ever.

"Are you the Devil?" I ask, pulling out the small crucifix that hangs around my neck.

The creature roars with laughter, and the lantern waves, bathing the darkness with its evanescent shining. The basilica dome amplifies the echoes of the guffaw, and I am about to pee on my pants. The hand that holds the cross shakes as if I was wielding a blender. This demon – or whatever it is – clearly doesn't fear the sacred symbol.

"Are you so arrogant as to think my Lord has no better things to do that coming here to talk with you?" The gargoyle shakes his bald head, frowning. "No, my dear cleric. You must get along with my presence here. And consider yourself fortunate, because you are the chosen one."

"The chosen one? What the fuck are you talking about? And what the hell is happening out there?"

It seems my swearwords please the creature. His smile broadens.

"Too many questions, too many questions... But I will answer them all in time. Walk with me."

"What if I say no?" I challenge.

The gargoyle shrugs.

"Maybe you'll stop being the chosen one. If I were you, I wouldn't make my Master angry."

"The chosen one? Chosen for what...?"

"All in good time," the gargoyle hisses. "Now, come outside with me, come on."

"But there's a battle going on outside! How can you keep those monsters away from me?"

He lifts the lantern, showing it to me.

"Stay close to the light and have no fear: no creature will harm you."

I don't trust this disgusting imp, but I know I have no choice.

"Do you have a name?" I finally ask.

"You can call me Absherim. And now, let's take a stroll."

I open the cathedral doors to be greeted by an unexpected view. The sky is now red. I don't know if it's because of all the fires that are burning down Barcelona or due to another darker reason. The clouds resemble blood clots hanging from above. I can see the wreckage of a fighter plane crashed into a building that is about to collapse. I cannot hear the symphony of screams any more. I am sure that most people are already dead. The pavement is also red, maybe dyed with the blood of the thousands of corpses that lie everywhere. When we leave the cathedral square, avoiding dead bodies, Absherim starts to talk:

"Stare at my Lord's vengeance, priest. This is what mankind deserves. Blame your paladin, Saint George, who killed the mortal form of my master when he dwelled the Earth."

"Your Lord?" I stop walking to light a cigarette, doubting as I do so that I will ever have a chance to finish off the pack. "But, who is your lord?"

"I think you have already guessed his name, but you are too scared to speak it." As the creature confirms my worst fear, I walk very close to him, trying to stay in the circle of light, even when there are not any winged or terrestrial monsters in sight. "My Lord has a lot of names: Lucifer, Satan, Iblis, Leviathan... Devil is his most popular definition. All this started long ago, when Lucifer asked God for a chance of redemption.

"Wait! Are you telling me the devil wanted to be forgiven?"

The monstrous dwarf laughs and shakes his head.

"You have ended up believing in your own lies: the eternal struggle between good and evil, God versus Devil, divine justice, infernal punishment... All that's rubbish, Chosen One. That's pure Manichaeism, invented by mankind." The creature carries on with his tale. "As I was saying, Lucifer asked for an audience with God, looking for redemption. What would you do if you were God, priest?"

"I think I would forgive him, because God is merciful."

"Ha! Maybe you are more merciful than your God, cleric. Your Lord did no better than issue a challenge in exchange for Lucifer's request: he required Lucifer to live amongst humans for a thousand years in peace, in the form of a ferocious red dragon. No matter how hard men hunted or tested him, he was not allowed to kill a single one, even in self-defence.

"But men are fearful, and the first sight of the beast flying over the woods and prairies made them take up arms against it. Lucifer was chased and hounded by a powerful warrior priest: George of Cappadocia. And your God cheated my Master, imbuing George's spear with his sacred power. Convinced that he would achieve redemption with his death, and in order to not break his pact with God, Lucifer did not defend himself against the warrior, suffering instead a deathblow that sent him back to Hell.

"Your words are hard to believe, Absherim..."

"Be silent, Chosen One, I have not finished," he commands. "But with the last breath of his mortal shape, Lucifer cast his final curse: at the appropriate time, all dragons, demons and beasts sculpted in the cities under Saint George's influence will come to life and destroy them. The sculptures would become vessels for his legions when they returned to Earth, to claim it as his new dominion.

"Hell on Earth," I mutter. "But is this happening just in Barcelona?"

"Oh, no, Chosen One. We are also conquering Cáceres, Aragón, the Balearic Islands... And those are just the Spanish cities under Saint George's protection. We are also obliterating England, Bulgaria, Portugal, Georgia, Ethiopia, Mali... The red sky will reign over them, and this is just the beginning. Lucifer plans to expand this destruction everywhere. This is the beginning of a new era: the age of demons, and the end of mankind.

"But why now, and not before?"

"Rage. Rage is the answer, my friend. Look around right now and you will see peace. Death is peaceful. Don't let the blood and fire confuse you. This is the end of the eternal conflict between religions, commanded by that entity you call God. Violence, bombing, killing, terrorism, xenophobia, homophobia, crime... Ask your Lord about it. Oh, excuse me, he never answers; he is always mute, too arrogant to listen to his sons' complaints. Have you ever called my Master? He always comes, as you should know."

Our walk takes us to the Sagrada Familia of Gaudí. I have smoked cigarette after cigarette, and now I am sure I will run out very soon. I can see lots of dragons, demons, gargoyles and basilisks around a big pile of corpses, in front of the most famous building of Barcelona. The stench of blood and burned flesh is nauseating. The red sky paints a horrifying picture. Small lightning flashes illuminate the crimson clouds. I light my last cigarette.

"We have arrived, Chosen One," the creature says, leaving the lantern on the ground. All the monsters stare at me and start roaring and hissing, in a dreadful cacophony. I am too scared to run away. "Smoke your cigarette and be joyful, because you will have the honour of receiving my Master."

"Your master? Do you mean Lucifer?"

Absherim raises his hand, and the fiery dragon-breath from a dozen reptilian mouths ignites the pyre. The flames rise high, and the roar reaches a crescendo. The column of fire climbs higher than the unfinished basilica towers, and a gigantic demonic figure starts to take shape around the bonfire.

I am terrified when I see the monsters lowering their heads as a sign of respect to me. Up high, the silhouette of the Master of Demons gains substance, revealing a fallen angel with infernal eyes, twisted horns and sharp teeth. His forefinger points at me, and then I realise why I am the chosen one.

I feel an indescribable pain when the Devil breaks through my body, raping my soul and burning my entrails. I scream, but my cry is replaced by a loud laugh. My eyes can see far beyond the horizon. My mind can now understand all the secrets of the universe. I am suffused by unlimited power. My last cigarette cannot please me anymore. My lungs are pure fire, and I love it.

You can call me Lucifer, Satan, Devil... Call it fortune.

Call it disgrace, if you are still alive. Earth is my new dominion, and I have a lot of things to do.

I am sure that somewhere, in heaven, God is weeping.

What Hungers
in the Dark

Aliette de Bodard

Cities are hungry.

Given a chance, cities will swallow you whole, reshape and twist you until you are part of their streets, part of their dreams and history. The older the city, the hungrier it is, the more used it has grown to eating its own neighbours – to swallow small villages and factories and forests until there is nothing left but a wider shopping street by the side of a metro station, an art centre with odd shapes, a small park drowned in the shadow of glass and metal buildings.

Generations of magicians in Lucía's family, and generations of loss. Old men, old women walking into parks and ghostly streets at the close of their lives; teenagers too sloppy to master the defensive arts, taking a wrong turn into an alleyway that twisted and closed around them; unborn babies in women's wombs, coming undone as their mothers, unaware of their existence, worked complicated and far-reaching spells, never realising what it was they had lost. And people who, early on, walked into the sea, into the streets, into the maws of metro stations – young, far too young.

Mami was forty-three years old when she lost her struggle with the city and forever vanished.

Forty-three. For nearly all of her life, Lucía has held that number against her chest like a talisman. Early. Too early.

Cities are hungry. But cities die, too, and in death they – at last, at long, long last – release their hold on what they've claimed.

Late one night, long after the last shuttles to spatioports have left, long after the last bunkers inland have filled up with the wealthy and the desperate, Lucía walks through el Barri Gòtic, to Poblenou. Past the half-drowned Parc de la Ciutadella – the zoo emptied of its animals, all the cages long since turned into shelters for fish and molluscs – past the Arc de Triomph, still unbowed and dry, a last survivor of the sea's onslaught.

In her childhood – such a long, long time ago it might as well be another country – Poblenou was a neighbourhood by the sea: a harbour, a beach, sun-drenched streets on a grid map, the clean, sharp smell of brine wafting into the street, the feel of Mami's hand in hers, a towering, reassuring presence that reminded Lucía everything was all right with the world.

Now, little of that left – Mami gone to her end decades ago, walking into the sea and becoming foam on the waves, sigh of the wind, seagulls' cries – the harbour at Port Olímpic and the beach drowned beneath the ever-rising water, Barceloneta a far-off peninsula, the streets cordoned off behind a seawall – half of them sacrificed so that the other might thrive, and then even that sacrifice becoming meaningless as more and more of the city was abandoned. Such a world they're bequeathing their children: a long, slow evacuation of cities and towns and villages, from houses to bunkers, from bunkers to shuttles and spacecraft, a slow relinquishing of a planet they've made unliveable in their rush to thrive.

Lucía stands, for a while, breathing in the smell of the sea: brine and the sharp smell of oil and pollutants, and the lights of strange, distorted fishes moving underwater. Her back and joints ache, the constant background to her days now, a low-grade pain that sometimes flares up into unbearable. The city spreads around and below her – not the strong presence it used to be, but a wounded beast, reeling from losses and bleeding its last beneath the dark clouds of pollution.

Almost time, then.

This far out, the network is erratic. The towers still self-repair, but the water has drowned half of them. When Lucía calls up her interface, it comes up static, giving her the emergency mode as it seeks to stabilise. No matter: the important messages are stored in her chip, where she can easily recall them.

One is a conversation between her and the children, a video of Sara and Ignacio in the desert near the space centre at Jiuquan. "I've thought about it, and I don't approve, Mama." Sara is not wearing her typical half-frown, the expression that used to amuse Lucía so much, looking at the world and dissecting it before coming to a decision, a trait that's really never left her. Her face is grave. "Ignacio doesn't approve, either."

They look well, though pale and drained. Away from the city that gave them power, they must endure weakness in the scant few months they have before they leave the planet – and then beyond that, build new ties, rebuild everything the family had, be the seed for generations of magicians drawing their power from domes and habitats on the Moon or on Mars or beyond. It will not be easy, or painless, but they are strong.

Sara's brother is silent, his hands hanging loosely at his side. When he does speak up, he's calmer than her. "It's your life. Your decision. And... I never knew her, so I can't tell."

Sara looks as though she's going to tell Ignacio off, but doesn't. "We're grown now." She picks her words slowly, carefully, her voice measured and tight, contracted around the tears she won't allow herself to shed. "That doesn't mean we don't need you. Come back to us, when you're done. Please."

"Best of luck, Mama," Ignacio says, looking up at the camera, smiling.

The world around Lucía has grown tight, too, unbearably light, like that moment when she watched Sara at three, trying to hand a plush giraffe to baby Ignacio and complaining that he wouldn't take it.

Come back to us.

"I'm sorry," she says, aloud.

Magic has only ever worked one way: blood for blood. A life for a life, for the city never gives anything for nothing.

The other video she calls up wasn't on her implants, originally. It started out in a format that's now obsolete, captured on a mobile phone, a contraption that went out of fashion more than forty years ago. Lucía has transferred it from phone to phone, from phone to glasses, and glasses to implants. It looks grainy and old-fashioned, in the way that film photographs did in her youth. It's brief: a woman holding a chubby-cheeked baby on her knees on a terrace on La Rambla del Poblenou, making small, indistinguishable conversation, and laughing at a joke someone makes, somewhere to the left of her. Then the baby, trying to catch something, spills horchata all over herself and starts bawling, and the woman cuddles her, whispering a lullaby, over and over, until the tears stop.

Lucía has other pictures and videos of Mami, but this is the one closest to the woman she remembers – to warmth, and songs, and stories, and a voice that always made the sun rise on her world.

Forty-three.

Lucía was nine when Mami walked into the sea at Platja del Bogatell. She left nothing behind her but clothes in a wardrobe, and a manuscript of unfinished chess problems that no one dared touch, Father unable to throw any of it away, clinging to the hope she would come back until it shrivelled him. Doctors spoke of depression, the police and the school of a tragic accident, the family of her time that had come, of how weak magicians always died young – nne of it helpful, none of it comforting – all of it *wrong*.

The video ends. Lucía replays it, again and again. She pauses, a fraction of a second longer than she should, on the last frames, on that barely audible lullaby Mami sings to baby

Lucía, scraps of words, snatches of tunes that have sunk into half-remembered memory.

Cities die.

Lucía would like to think of something sharp and meaningful to say, but her mind is as desolate as the city around her. Its presence is no longer the sharp, hungry one she's always worked with, the beast that must be placated and sated, but something small and diminished, whimpering.

Lucía breathes, taking the soul of the city deep into herself. She stands on the seawall, at the boundary between the sea and the buildings – not the boundary of the city, because things take time to set in stone, because the memory of bright, vivid marketplaces, of narrow streets where children like Lucía once held their mothers' hands, is stronger than even decades of being buried under foam and waves.

She feels it throb and contort within her, feels every wound, every hurt: the airport town of El Prat de Llobregat evacuated, the network of metros flooded, the factories of la Zona Franca now silent and lost, most of Sant Adrià del Besos and Badalo forever drowned beneath the sea, with Sant Adrià's three disaffected industrial chimneys rising towards the heavens in a last defiance, useless spears of rusted and corroded metal.

Ssh. There, there. Over and over, as if she were soothing an infant to sleep. It's instinct, and it's wrong, as wrong as the explanations they gave for Mami's death. The city shouldn't be weak. It shouldn't seek comfort. It shouldn't... It shouldn't be *pliant*, bowing at the mere sound of her voice, shouldn't feel as though the slightest push will send it crumbling.

There are steps, in the seawall, leading down to the oily waves. Lucía walks down one flight, stops. The city sloshes within her, quietly sobbing, reaching out for her thoughts, for her soul, like a child for a flame. Lucía keeps it separate from herself effortlessly – not even a need for wards, she could push it almost all the way out, at the edge that Aunt

Dolores always said was the unattainable ideal – the city almost out of the magician's mind, its hunger muted and defanged, but its power still flowing through the body.

There, there.

She's not quite sure why she's weeping.

Beneath her are buildings and streets, hidden within the darkness of the sea, but the city calls to them, outlines them in traceries of light: Carrer d'Avila, Carrer de Rosa Sensat, Avinguda d'Icària... All the familiar intersections of her childhood that she would run across with the weight of her schoolbooks at her back, tucking both hands under the curve of her backpack to stop the straps from digging into her shoulders; the longer line of La Rambla del Poblenou where Mami and Papa and Lucía used to walk under the trees on the Sunday before queuing for ice cream at the oldest orxateria in the neighbourhood – and, further on, the wide curve of the beach where Mami vanished.

Mami.

Please, she says, to the city, thinking of a dark-haired, round-faced woman with freckles on her tanned skin – Father always used to say she'd get skin cancer if she continued to stay out at the hottest hours of the day, but Mami loved the sun too much – of songs and lullabies and indefinable warmth. *Give her back.*

It fights her, of course. Mami is foam and waves and the wrecks of boats, subsumed into the sand, the hotels, the harbour. She's myth and legend, the woman who drowned, the mother who abandons her own child, part of the city's history, and the city never ever lets go of what has been woven into its fabric.

But, in the end, the city is weaker than her.

Light climbs, from the water, coalesces slowly into the shape of a body – pass after pass, as if some ineffable being were drawing with a pen made of a thousand stars, a thousand moons. Lucía doesn't look down, not at her own hands, which will have started to fade, or at her shadow in the moonlight, which is shrivelling and vanishing. The world feels stretched, hurtful, too bright, too intense. If she intended to survive this, now would be the time to break it off, to walk away before losing herself.

But, of course, surviving was never the point.

The outline is now that of a woman, the face in shadow but the pose heartbreakingly familiar.

"Lucía?" her voice is the whisper of the wind on the sand.

Breathing hurts, now. So close. Just a few more minutes. Just a few more moments of coaxing the city into giving her what she wants. So close. "Mami. I –" Lucía fights back tears. "I waited so long."

The face is just shadows, and the being she's summoned cocks her head this way and that, her long hair still trailing into the sea – no, not the sea, its strands are flowing seamlessly into the water, a thousand thousand dark threads linking her to the drowned streets, the rusted buildings. "Your life for mine." A silence. The world around Lucía is dark now, colourless, the city opening out its arms to her – starving, given a far richer meal than it ever expected – come with me, Lucía, come and never be alone anymore.

Lucía swallows, struggling for words that seem to have fled. Mami – the being that should be Mami – Is distant and alien, unbearably emotionless at being brought back. "You were a magician. You know that's how it works. You can't give away something –" She can't feel her arms or legs any more. All that seems to be left is the sound of her own heartbeat, the burning of polluted air in her lungs. She takes her pain, slowly, carefully starts to weave it into the blade that will cut those last threads linking Mami to the city, that will make her whole.

In the silence, Mami's voice is a gunshot. "You're not ready." The tone – Lucía is seven again, being sent to bed early, or far younger, told off because she threw a temper tantrum – stubborn pride at drawing Mami's attention, burning shame at disappointing her.

"I am." She's done with her life, really. Raised her

children and sent them away, buried her wife in Montjuïc on the other side of the mountain from their flat, lived alone in a doomed city for months, steeling herself for her last and greatest spell.

In Lucía's hand is a plain fisherman's knife, its blade long and thin and sharp, so sharp it's dug into her palm and left a long trail of blood, a pain she barely feels. "You have to come, Mami."

"Why would I?" Mami shakes her head. "This isn't the way things work." And it's not her speaking. It's the city – wind in corroded buildings, asphalt cracking under the heat, the beats between words the silence of desolate flats and empty plastic chairs on sidewalks.

No. No.

It's not only the threads that bind her to the city, not only the hair and the sea. What Lucía has cobbled up looks like Mami now, not like a child's drawing or a high-concept sketch on someone's implants, but her legs are the colour of the slick cobblestones she stands on – and when she cocks her head, bits and pieces of the city flash in her eyes: the ruined zoo cages, the narrow, yellow buildings of the Barri Gòtic, the destroyed metros in flooded tunnels.

She's failed.

"You're not her," she says, slowly, softly, her blood mingling with the oil-spills on the cobblestones.

"Only in part." Mami's face – *its* face – is in shadows again, unreadable. Inhuman. "I was lost years ago, corazón. You have to let go."

The city. She's summoned the city and its endless hunger, given it flesh and bones, and enough strength to reach out and gobble Lucía whole. She's lost: finally, irretrievably lost – a beginner's mistake, too far gone to be undone. She –

No.

But, when the being she's summoned lifts a hand to touch her, it does so slowly, hesitantly, its face twisted into a familiar grimace, that of Mami steeling herself for something unpleasant. "I will not," it says, stiffly. "You've lost enough." And walks back towards the sea, its shape already scattering and fading, going back to nothingness. In Lucía's mind, the pressing need, the pressing hunger of the city, diminishes and finally dies away. It's leaving her there on the steps with water staining her trousers, withdrawing from her – a wounded animal, Lucía suddenly sees with merciless clarity, going to curl up in a corner and die. Going to fade away, drained of everything that once made it vibrant and alive and *hungry*.

Lucía's heart breaks, all over again. "Wait," she says.

It's going away from her, the threads that tie it back to the sea shortening and fading, just as its body is fading. "It's for the best, corazón."

"You're dying," she says. It doesn't answer. Of course it's dying. Of course that's the only way the city would ever allow Lucía to wrestle it for control, for reparations. "There –" She swallows, tasting bile, tasting blood. "There is a way."

She holds out the knife, handle first, feeling its weight and heft in the palm of her hand.

It's turned, on the edge of the sea, watching her. Its face is Mami's, trying to work out a chess problem; Grandmother's, as she faced down the entire family at Great-Uncle Feliu's funeral; other people that she's only seen in videos and faded pictures; and something else, too, the glass windows of trains, the facades of tapas bars and restaurants, the ochre-and-blue mosaics of Parc Güell.

"Please."

"I would have devoured you, in other circumstances." The voice is almost amused. It's entirely gone from her thoughts now – no rush of power or sensation that she hovers on the edge of some abyss. "Just as I took the others."

Of course it would have. Of course that's its nature, what it's always done, how it's always worked. Of course… Of course it took Mami as it would have taken Lucía and

Ignacio and Sara (and the thought of her children disappearing and dying is more painful than that of her own end). She should be glad to see it go, to see it finally getting its just desserts.

Except... Except that her heart feels broken and hollow, grieving for a loss so large she can barely encompass all of it.

Lucía holds out the knife again, wordlessly. At length it moves, smooth and elegant and utterly inhuman, reaching out to take the weight of the blade from her. It raises the knife, draws the blade across the curves of its hair, as casually as discarding a too-large jumper or a coat. Lucía feels... a slight jolt, in her hands, a reminder that she originally fashioned the blade – but the power, in the end, doesn't come from her or anything that she does, not any more.

You have to let go.

Thread after thread, falling back into the sea – fading, ghostly and crystalline, and the buildings around them turning... grey, insignificant, as if clouds were rushing across their surface to blot out sunlight and moonlight. At length, it stands, dropping what's left of the knife on the cobblestones – a splash, as the remnant hits the water and sinks into the drowned streets. Lucía can hear the sound of its breath as it bows down to her: the exhaust of cars, the rush of metros, the intangible noise of crowds on Plaça de Catalunya.

"Thank you," it says. It stands dark and tall, skin the colour of steel girders, the curve of wrought-iron balconies on its arms; and around it, spread on the floor like the cloth of a shadowy skirt, are familiar shapes – metros, marketplaces, sand and sea, ruined churches and devastated apartment blocks.

"Where –" she tastes blood and bile on her tongue again. "Where will you go?"

It shrugs. "Where I can." It moves, then, with that same odd smoothness – hands trailing into her hair, lightly, as it passes her, a goodbye or a blessing or both, something that should have been unbearably heavy but isn't.

Lucía, still kneeling in the water, watches it go, the memory of its touch like a ghost's kiss, numbing and exhilarating at the same time.

She thinks of it – of the city, of part of it, of all that's left – carrying memories of dead places and of the dead like dandelion seeds; walking in that same smooth and steady way out of the devastation, into a strange and uncertain future.

Barcelona/My Love

Elia Barceló

"Barcelona" – I said when It asked, and I still don't know why.

Barcelona is a beautiful city, sure, and I had lived there for almost a year when I was writing my master thesis and had been reasonably happy, but there was nothing special there for me, no love lost, no bittersweet memories, not even any friends I could have visited. I said "Barcelona" probably because I just didn't like the idea of going back to my hometown and having to meet everyone again, not after what had happened to me and shortly before what was going to happen to everybody else. I didn't want to be a tourist either, seeing the sights in London, Venice, New York, Singapore or Angkor Wat, spending my last two weeks in the old world in exotic places I had never been to. I could have, of course. It asked where I wanted to start and I could have named any town. So I said Barcelona.

It was September, a lovely month on the Mediterranean coast: warm temperatures, tanned, relaxed, smiling women after the summer holidays, *verbenas* all over the place every night, the scent of flowers and the smells of food, the deep blue sea, the language of my childhood, my mother tongue... basic things I had almost forgotten.

I had been away for over thirty years, although when I looked in the mirror of the hotel room on my first night back I looked the same, exactly as It had promised. What wasn't the same was the rest. I mean the world. It was much, much worse.

I could say this came as a shock to me, but I would be lying; there was no shock, I had almost expected it. Or maybe I should say it was sort of a small nasty shock, but not a surprise. I expected the world to be a mess and so it was. The gap between rich and poor had grown even more enormous, the power of organized religions and its influence on human behavior had returned to the extent of the Middle Ages, the violence was indescribable, the ignorance of the population – now that basic education was compulsory in most countries – had risen exponentially. People thought they knew everything because now they had mobile phones and the Internet. I had always loathed my species and what they had done to our planet but now, after thirty years living with It in a sensible environment, the truth was clearer than ever: we were destroying the Earth and destroying ourselves in the process. It had to come to an end. Humankind wasn't capable of inhabiting our planet properly.

"It is time to start," It had said and that was the way I saw things too. After living together for so long I had at last abandoned the idea that deciding the future of an entire planet on my own was a problem. My species was wrong. The *other* species – It – was right. The decision was perfectly logical: It should take over, stop the catastrophe and put us back on the right track.

For three decades now I had been exposed to Its/their way of thinking, the way It/they did things. I had learned their only language – or more than their language, their way of communicating with one another – they had learned mine and, together, we had decided to save the world, my world.

It was now six o'clock in the afternoon on the tenth day of my stay. I was sitting in the shade at a small café in front of the Liceu, Barcelona's famous opera house, watching the people strolling up and down the Rambla: the street artists, the beggars, the thieves, inhaling the pungent smell of a human city, drinking a *carajillo* – strong coffee laced with cognac – and thinking what would all my fellow men and women say if they knew I was on the verge of – so to say – signing the world over to an alien species. I could picture the outraged faces of all of the world's politicians – democrats and tyrants equally – at the idea of not having been consulted about it, and I had to laugh aloud. No referendums needed, no elections, no polls.

It thought that I was a valid representative of my species – that I *was* in fact my species – and that therefore I had the right of speaking for them all. It was a great feeling and, now that my qualms had passed, it felt marvelous to be about to do the right thing.

I drank the last drops of my coffee, paid, and strolled down towards the sea, toward the high column where poor Columbus points perpetually in the direction of America, the New World. Suddenly I felt the urge to visit the Pueblo Español, where scaled-down reproductions of several Spanish monuments and cities are housed. The visit could pass for a farewell to my country in general as well as a nostalgic tour of the past.

I took the cable car and, suspended over the harbor, had a lovely view of Barcelona, lying like a giant colorful tapestry from the Tibidabo to the sea. Something forgotten stirred in me at seeing the tiny houses, the tiny cars, the ant-like people busily moving about, doing incomprehensible things. Pity? Tenderness? There were so many words I had forgotten... Probably many feelings, too. I was still human; of course I was. But sometimes... maybe not quite. Thirty years is a long time for a human being.

In Montjuich the narrow streets of cobblestone were shaded, twisted, mysterious, full of small shops which were just opening for the evening, of romantic restaurants for couples on holiday or on honeymoon; bushes of bougainvillea exploded on corners where you could catch a glimpse of the sea, the heat came up from the stones and mingled with the scent of jasmine and other plants I couldn't put a name to. A young woman in a pale blue summer dress was taking a picture of a patio through the black iron bars of the gate. She had pushed her sunglasses up like a hairband for her chestnut reddish hair and was smiling at her camera, lost in the pleasure of doing something she loved.

On impulse, I looked on the Internet and phoned the small restaurant by the sea I used to go to as a student. If I could get a table for the evening, I would talk to her and treat her to dinner.

"For tonight? Do you really mean you want a table for tonight, at the terrace?" I might as well have said I wanted to fly to the moon. "Sorry. We are fully booked till November. Would the 3rd of December suit you?"

I didn't answer. They would be out of business in December; I knew for sure.

I pocketed my new prepaid mobile phone and went to talk to the girl anyway.

"So you are a writer," said the girl – Natalia – after we had finished our dessert in a small restaurant in Gràcia. "Tell me a story, then. A story of something that happened to you. Something special."

I smiled at her. I had told her I was a writer because it wasn't so far from the truth. I had had two stories published in a science fiction fanzine a long time ago, before my life with It.

Her eyes were sparkling. She was very pretty in a funny way: her hazel eyes were too wide apart, her nose too small, her mouth too big, but the effect was stunning, nonetheless. After thinking about it I decided that she was beautiful because she was so very much alive.

"Well, I could tell you how thirty years ago I was abducted by aliens," I said.

"Oh, yes, do. It sounds really exciting. Shall we have another bottle of this fantastic wine?"

"Of course." I lifted the bottle and signaled the waiter for another.

"It happened on the 8th of August, thirty one years ago," I started. "I was twenty seven." Her smile grew brighter, appreciating the big lie she thought I was concocting for her. "That means you are almost sixty now," she said. I nodded and kept on talking. "I was driving back from a party which had been held in one of the small towns near Madrid, where I was living at the time, at three in the morning. The road was empty and dark. It was one of these small local winding roads that crosses through the hills. A beautiful starry night. I remember I lit a cigarette, inhaled and felt suddenly happy for no reason. Just to be alive, to be driving through the hills on a summer night with no responsibilities nor anybody waiting for me at my flat because I was single again, having left my girlfriend a couple of months before. It was a perfect moment.

An then, just as I drove out of the trees and started to descend towards the valley, I saw a light, a very bright orange light that blinded me for a moment. I braked like a madman, swerved to the right, and covered my eyes with my hands. After a few seconds I peeked through my fingers and saw a... How can I describe it? A sort of a weird airplane suspended in the air in front of me. It looked like one of these old pictures of a UFO, but this time, incredibly, it was real, real as life and twice as beautiful.

The craft hovered soundlessly in front of me radiating a light that was also a sound... A kind of music, and at the same time a warm caress, like velvet or silk, orange, amber, crimson, something pulsating as if it were alive. I felt it scan me but, strangely, that didn't feel like an invasion of privacy; it was more like what a blind person might do when she touches you to know who you are.

After a long time, it... they... asked me if I wanted to go with them... to go travelling with them. And I said yes. That was thirty one years ago."

"So you just came back. Or have you been here longer?"

"I just came back. You are the first human I've spoken with. I mean, not counting waiters and hotel receptionists."

"What did they want from you?"

"The waiters?"

"No, silly. The aliens."

"Oh, nothing. They just wanted to get to know us."

"That implies they think that if they know you, they

know us humans in general, as a species. That's a bit simple, isn't it? You'll have to work on that, Mr. Writer; your readers aren't going to accept it. These aliens are supposed to be intelligent, aren't they?"

"Yes. Very. Much more than we are."

"Keep working on it." She smiled again and drank all the wine that was left in her glass. I poured her another one.

"It's a nice story."

"It's the truth."

"Sure. And they lived happily ever after, didn't they?"

"That's the idea."

"Great. I like happy endings."

I walked her to her hotel thinking all the time if I should try to go up with her to her room. I hadn't had physical sex with anyone for over thirty years and I didn't even know if sex would be an option in the new order of things. Reproduction was not, in any case; I knew that for sure, we – It and myself – had discussed the subject and agreed on that. Our planet was already overpopulated.

This could be my last chance to have sex, but I didn't want Natalia to think I was desperate. Though maybe I was.

"Shall we meet tomorrow?" she asked by the hotel door.

"I'll pick you up at ten and we can have breakfast together. I haven't had *churros* for ages."

"Being with the aliens and all that." She gave me that impish smile again.

We kissed lightly on the lips and suddenly I knew I didn't want to hurry. No way was I going to miss the opportunity to court this girl, falling slowly for her, making her mine. I needed time and, although I didn't know how, I was going to get it. I had to talk to It.

I still had four days left before It started to change things in my planet which now, suddenly, since I had started to date Natalia, didn't look so bad any more. Obviously the main frame hadn't changed at all: the poor kept getting poorer, the rich richer; genocides and massacres with or without religious justifications kept going on; climate and general ecologic condition kept deteriorating, that was all true.

But, at the same time, Barcelona was more beautiful with every minute, people were extremely nice to us – I had forgotten how nice humans can be with a couple in love like we were – the sun was bright, the sea was incredibly blue, the nights long and warm and silvery. I kept wishing this state of bliss could last forever, but I had made a promise to It, and even if I hadn't, I knew – my mind, my brain knew – that it was all for the best, that giving It the dominion over our world was the intelligent thing to do, the only way to save the planet.

It was just... that I wasn't that enthusiastic anymore. When It started the big changes, love was bound to disappear, being one of the main forces acting on humans, probably even the main source of incomprehensible and incontrollable behavior on our part, something It couldn't allow to continue.

Yes, I know this sounds a bit cheesy, but I didn't want to imagine a planet were love didn't exist at all, where something such as Natalia and I were experiencing would be considered an illness, plain madness, a condition that required curing.

When I was living with It/them, none of this had mattered; it didn't seem important if people were allowed to fall in love or not. I had forgotten how great this feeling was, how human, how central to our way of being alive and part of the universe. I really didn't know what to do because I was almost sure I couldn't go back on my word but at the same time I knew I wasn't going to renounce Natalia. I had even started to think about our future as a couple, as a family. Did I want my children to grow up in a world ruled by It? It was undoubtedly for the best. Only... it wouldn't be human anymore. And – a stupid little detail I had forgotten – children had no place in the next future, not for the next sixty of eighty years in all likelihood.

During these last four days – often as I was walking hand in hand with Natalia through the streets of Barcelona, kissing on the Tibidabo, laughing on top of the weird towers of Gaudi's incredible cathedral – I would think that the end of the world as I had known it was nothing but a fantasy, something I had dreamed while lying in a hospital in a coma. I couldn't believe everything was coming to an end and this gorgeous city was going to change for ever.

Sometimes I tried to comfort myself thinking that when it finally happened I would also be changed as planned and I would merge with It/them so that I would turn into It and in effect become the ruler of the Earth. But I wouldn't be quite myself anymore. And precisely that, which had seemed such an excellent idea while I was living with It/them on Its/their planet, wasn't so attractive anymore; because now that I loved Natalia I wanted to keep being myself, just plain old me.

I thought about discussing the whole thing with her but I knew her well enough: she was passionate, stubborn and always ready to fight for her ideals. She would never allow It to take control if she could help it, and if I insisted... I would lose her.

She still didn't know the truth. We had made love on the second day, but not even then, in bed together, in the afterglow of our glorious lovemaking, had I been able to tell her what was going to happen. I was too scared of losing her.

I kept torturing myself. What did I want? What was the right thing to do? What could I possibly do to avoid hurting her, myself or anyone else? Should I just go on with the plan, suffer the big change and simply hope that I didn't come to regret it? It was difficult to analyze the situation as I used to when I was alone, far from the Earth. Things kept getting entangled in my mind: thoughts, feelings, fantasies, plans, dreams, consequences...

What was best for the world? The answer was It. That much was clear.

What was the best for me? Natalia. Me and Natalia in Barcelona, in late summer, at the beginning of our love affair.

Suddenly, the solution occurred to me, and like all perfect solutions it was incredibly simple. Just a touch egoistic maybe, but in love and war...

On the last day before the change I went to talk to It and It agreed with my plan.

"Do you think we can get a table again at that lovely restaurant by the sea?" Natalia asked as she was brushing her hair in front of the mirror. She was dressed in white, Ibiza style, and her belly was just starting to show.

"We can try." She had been overwhelmed the first time I had taken her there; it was a very romantic place. I dialed.

"Mr. Escribano, what a pleasure! Of course! This evening, eight thirty, our best table for our best customer."

I smiled, feeling happy. I also loved that little place with the great food.

"Do you want to take a taxi or shall we walk?" I asked Natalia.

"I'd rather walk. The weather is so fine... We are having a perfect September, don't you think?"

We went out and as I turned the key to lock the palace we were living in –the Palau Güell, near the Liceu – I thought fleetingly about the other Barcelona, the one ruled by It on the original Earth. Were they happy in the new world, under the new order? Probably. I had been reasonably satisfied for thirty one years.

But this was something else. This was my real life: Natalia, the baby we were going to have, an eternal summer, the most beautiful city in the world just for the three of us. Barcelona and our love.

About the Authors

Elia Barceló (1957) is a Spanish academic and author. Born in Elda, in the Alicante province, Barceló earned her doctorate in Innsbruck in 1995. She is now a Professor of Spanish literature in Austria. She is a multiple award-winning author of science fiction and YA novels, and has been cited as the most important female SF author writing in Spanish. Her work has been translated into eighteen languages, including English language editions of her novels *Heart of Tango* and *The Goldsmith's Secret*.

Aliette de Bodard lives and works in Paris. She is the author of the critically acclaimed Obsidian and Blood trilogy of Aztec noir fantasies, as well as numerous short stories. Recent works include *The House of Shattered Wings* (Roc/Gollancz, 2015 British Science Fiction Association Award), a novel set in a turn-of-the-century Paris devastated by a magical war, and its upcoming sequel *The House of Binding Thorns* (April 2017, Roc/Gollancz). She also published *The Citadel of Weeping Pearls* (Asimov's Oct/Nov 2015), a novella set in the same universe as her Vietnamese space opera *On a Red Station Drifting*.

Alberto M. Caliani (Ceuta, Spain, 1963) is the author of the adventure thriller *El Secreto de Boca Verde* (winner of the 2013 Pandemia Award for best fiction novel) and the historical novel *La Conspiración del Rey Muerto* (ed. Palabras de Agua). He has also contributed stories to many Spanish horror anthologies. His new book, *La Iglesia* (*The Church*), a demonic horror novel, will be published in the first quarter of 2017.

Dave Hutchinson was born in Sheffield in 1960. Once upon a time, he was a journalist, but now he's not. He is the author of six collections of short stories and three novels. His latest collection, *Sleeps With Angels*, is available from NewCon Press. His novels *Europe in Autumn* and *Europe at Midnight* were both shortlisted for the BSFA, Arthur C Clarke, and John W Campbell Memorial

Awards, and his novella *The Push* (also NewCon Press) was shortlisted for the BSFA Award. A third *Europe* book, *Europe in Winter*, is to be published in November 2016. He lives in North London.

Claude Lalumière (claudepages.info) is the author of *Objects of Worship*, *The Door to Lost Pages*, *Nocturnes and Other Nocturnes*, and (forthcoming in 2017) *Venera Dreams*. His first fiction appeared in *Interzone* in 2002, and he has since published more than 100 stories; his work has been translated into French, Italian, Polish, Spanish, and Serbian. In summer 2016, he was one of 21 international short fiction writers showcased at Serbia's Kikinda Short 11: The New Deal.

Rodolfo Martínez (Asturias, Spain, 1965) is a computer programmer and one of the most prolific science fiction writers in Spain. Notable works include cyberpunk novels *La sonrisa del gato* (1995), available in English as *Cat's Whirld*, and *El sueño del rey rojo* (2004), the Ignotus-winning space opera *Tierra de nadie: Jormundgand* [No Man's Land: Jormungand], the 2005 urban fantasy *Los sicarios del cielo* [Heaven's Hired Assassins], which won a Minotauro Award, *Fieramente humano* [Fiercely Human] in 2011, which won another Ignotus Award, and the series El adepto de la reina (2009), available in English as *The Queen's Adept*. Martínez also runs independent publishing house Sportula.

Virginia Pérez de la Puente's first novel, *Chosen by Death* (Ediciones B, 2010), was described as "the best Spanish fantasy debut of the century." It introduced her saga The Second Havoc, which continued with the novels *The Dream of the Dead* (Minotauro, 2013), *Between the Two Shores* (2014), *Fate's Puppets* (2016) and the novellas *Dreaming about Forests* (2013) and *My Soul for my King* (2014). In 2015 she published a standalone novel, *Children of the One-Eyed God*, a twist on classic Nordic mythology. Her novels frequently appear on lists of the best fantasy books of the year.

Sofía Rhei (Madrid, 1978) is an experimental speculative author, with more than thirty titles published. Her books for children include the series Krippys (Montena), *El joven Moriarty* (Fábulas de

Albión) and *Los hermanos Mozart* (Diquesí), as well as many stand-alone titles such as *Olivia Shakespeare* (Edelvives) and *La calle Andersen* (La Galera) co-written with Marian Womack. Her YA novels include *Flores de sombra* (Alfaguara) and its sequel *Savia negra*. As a poet, she was shortlisted for the Dwarf Star and Rhysling awards. Her first novel for adults is *Róndola* (Minotauro), a humorous fairytale retelling. Find out more at Sofiarhei.com

Sarah Singleton is the author of the contemporary fantasy novel *The Crow Maiden* and eight novels for young adults, including *Century* (Booktrust Teen Award 2005), *Heretic* and *The Amethyst Child*, all published by Simon & Schuster UK. She has published many stories in magazines and anthologies, including *Interzone*, *Black Static* and *The Dark*. Sarah has worked as a journalist and a secondary school teacher of English. She lives in Wiltshire, England, county of long barrows, stone circles and white horses

Lisa Tuttle has been writing horror, fantasy and science fiction since the 1970s. Her first collection of horror stories, *A Nest of Nightmares*, was published as *Nido de Pesadillas* by Fabulas de Albion in 2015. Her first novel, *Windhaven*, written in collaboration with George R.R. Martin and first published in 1981, is also available in Spanish (*Refugio del Viento*, published by Gigamesh). Her most recent novel is the first in a series of supernatural detective stories set in the 1890s, *The Curious Affair of the Somnambulist and the Psychic Thief*. She lives in Scotland.

Born in 1943, **Ian Watson** has by now authored a baker's dozen of story collections, most recently *The 1000 Year Reich* (NewCon Press, 2016). Since 2010 he has lived in a seaside town in the north of Spain, and is married to the translator of the *Game of Thrones* books (and much else), Cristina Macía, with whom he has so far co-authored a cookbook of historic recipes. Upcoming in 2017 from NewCon Press will be his technothriller *Waters of Destiny* (with Andy West) about how a 12th century Arab doctor of genius could realistically have identified the true cause of the Black Death and stored it with horrifying repercussions nowadays.

Ian Whates is a writer and editor of science fiction, fantasy, and horror. The author of six novels (three space opera and three urban fantasy with steampunk overtones), the co-author of two more (military SF), he has seen nearly seventy of his short stories published in a variety of venues and has edited some thirty anthologies. His work has been shortlisted for the Philip K Dick Award and twice for BSFA Awards. Ian also runs multiple award-winning independent publisher NewCon Press, which he founded by accident in 2006. He is a director of the BSFA (British Science Fiction Association), an organisation he chaired for five years.

Marian Womack is a graduate of the Clarion Writers Workshop (2014), and of the Creative Writing Master's at the University of Cambridge (2016). She was born in Andalusia and writes in English and Spanish. Her fiction in English can be read in *Apex*, *SuperSonic Mag*, *Weird Fiction Review*, and the anthologies *Spanish Women of Wonder* (2016) and *The Year's Best Weird Fiction*, vol. 3 (2016). She has also published non-fiction in *The Times Literary Supplement*, *The Science-Fiction and Fantasy Network*, and has written for video-games. Her work as a translator can be read in *The Apex Book of World SF* (vol. 4; ed. Mahvesh Murad), *Castles in Spain* (ed. Sue Burke) and *The Big Book of SF* (ed. Ann & Jeff VanderMeer). She co-runs Ediciones Nevsky/Nevsky Books, a small press based in Madrid and Cambridge, specialising in European & Spanish slipstream in translation. She tweets as @beekeepermadrid and her website is marianwomack.com

NEWCON PRESS

Publishing quality Science Fiction, Fantasy, Dark Fantasy and Horror for ten years and counting.

Winner of the 2010 'Best Publisher' Award from the European Science Fiction Society.

Anthologies, novels, short story collections, novellas, paperbacks, hardbacks, signed limited editions, e-books…
Why not take a look at some of our other titles?

Featured authors include:
Neil Gaiman, Brian Aldiss, Kelley Armstrong, Peter F. Hamilton, Alastair Reynolds, Stephen Baxter, Christopher Priest, Tanith Lee, Joe Abercrombie, Dan Abnett, Nina Allan, Sarah Ash, Neal Asher, Tony Ballantyne, James Barclay, Chris Beckett, Lauren Beukes, Aliette de Bodard, Chaz Brenchley, Keith Brooke, Eric Brown, Pat Cadigan, Jay Caselberg, Michael Cobley, Genevieve Cogman, Storm Constantine, Hal Duncan, Jaine Fenn, Paul di Filippo, Jonathan Green, Jon Courtenay Grimwood, Frances Hardinge, Gwyneth Jones, M. John Harrison, Amanda Hemingway, Paul Kane, Leigh Kennedy, Nancy Kress, Kim Lakin-Smith, David Langford, Alison Littlewood, James Lovegrove, Una McCormack, Ian McDonald, Sophia McDougall, Gary McMahon, Ken MacLeod, Ian R MacLeod, Gail Z. Martin, Juliet E. McKenna, John Meaney, Simon Morden, Mark Morris, Anne Nicholls, Stan Nicholls, Marie O'Regan, Philip Palmer, Stephen Palmer, Sarah Pinborough, Gareth L. Powell, Robert Reed, Rod Rees, Andy Remic, Mike Resnick, Mercurio D. Rivera, Adam Roberts, Justina Robson, Stephanie Saulter, Gaie Sebold, Robert Shearman, Sarah Singleton, Martin Sketchley, Kari Sperring, Brian Stapleford, Charles Stross, Tricia Sullivan, E.J. Swift, David Tallerman, Adrian Tchaikovsky, Steve Rasnic Tem, Lavie Tidhar, Lisa Tuttle, Simon Kurt Unsworth, Ian Watson, Freda Warrington, Liz Williams, Neil Williamson, and many more.

Join our mailing list to get advance notice of new titles, book launches and events, and receive special offers on books:
www.newconpress.co.uk

Now We Are Ten
Commemorating the First 10 Years
Edited by Ian Whates
Peter F. Hamilton, Nancy Kress, Ian McDonald, Genevieve Cogman, Adrian Tchaikovsky and more...

To celebrate NewCon Press' tenth birthday, some of the world's finest science fiction and fantasy authors were invited to write new stories inspired by the number, divisions, or multiples of: ten. The results were remarkable...

Released July 2016. Available as a signed limited edition hardback, paperback, and eBook.

Cover art by Ben Baldwin

Contents:
Introduction by Ian Whates
The Final Path – Genevieve Cogman
Women's Christmas – Ian McDonald
Pyramid – Nancy Kress
Liberty Bird – Jaine Fenn
Zanzara Island – Rachel Armstrong
Ten Sisters – Eric Brown
Licorice – Jack Skillingstead
The Time Travellers' Ball (A Story in Ten Words) – Rose Biggin
Dress Rehearsal – Adrian Tchaikovsky
The Tenth Man – Bryony Pearce
Rare as a Harpy's Tear – Neil Williamson
How to Grow Silence from Seed – Tricia Sullivan
Utopia +10 – JA Christy
Ten Love Songs to Change the World – Peter F Hamilton
Ten Days – Nina Allan
Front Row Seat to the End of the World – EJ Swift

www.newconpress.co.uk

Ten Tall Tales
And Twisted Limericks
Edited by Ian Whates

**Ramsey Campbell, Michael Marshall Smith,
Sarah Pinborough, James Barclay,
Lynda E. Rucker, Edward Cox** and more…

Produced in celebration of NewCon Press' 10th anniversary. Ten Tall Tales of horror, dark fantasy and dark science fiction, commissioned from some of the most twisted imaginations writing today. Each story is inter-leafed with a Twisted Limerick from that master of terror, Ramsey Campbell.

Contents:

Released July 2016. Available as a signed limited edition hardback, paperback, and eBook.

Immanion Press

Speculative Fiction

Dark in the Day, Ed. by Storm Constantine & Paul Houghton

Weirdness lurks beyond the margins of the mundane, emerging to dismantle our assumptions of reality. Dark in the Day is an anthology of weird fiction, penned by established writers and also those new to the genre – the latter being authors who are, or were, students of Creative Writing at Staffordshire University, where editor Storm Constantine occasionally delivers guest lectures. Her co-editor, Paul Houghton, is the senior lecturer in Creative Writing at the university.

Contributors include: Martina Bellovičová, J. E. Bryant, Glynis Charlton, Storm Constantine, Louise Coquio, Elizabeth Counihan, Krishan Coupland, Elizabeth Davidson, Siân Davies, Paul Finch, Rosie Garland, Rhys Hughes, Kerry Fender, Andrew Hook, Paul Houghton, Tanith Lee, Tim Pratt, Nicholas Royle, Michael Marshall Smith, Paula Wakefield, Ian Whates and Liz Williams.

ISBN: 978-1-907737-74-9 £11.99, $18.99

Animate Objects by Tanith Lee

There is no such thing as an inanimate object… And how could that be? Because, simply, everything is formed from matter, and basically, at *root*, the matter that makes up everything in the physical world – the Universe – is of the same substance. Which means, on that basic level, we – you, me, and that power station over there – are all the exact riotous, chaotic, amorphous *same*. Here is an assortment of Lee takes on the nature, and perhaps intentions, of so-called non-sentient things. And you're quite safe. This is only a book. An inanimate object.

From the Introduction by Tanith Lee

The original hardback of this collection, of which there were only 35 copies, was published by Immanion Press in 2013, to commemorate Tanith Lee receiving the Lifetime Achievement Award at World Fantasycon. It included 5 previously unpublished pieces. This new release includes a further 2 stories, co-written by Tanith Lee and John Kaiine, and new interior illustrations by Jarod Mills.

ISBN: 978-1-907737-73-2, £11.99 $18.99

Lightning Source UK Ltd.
Milton Keynes UK
UKOW02n1435131016

285199UK00004B/12/P

9 781910 935279